D0621891

SWERVE
(A Novel Divergence)

Vincent James / Rowland Saifi / McCormick Templeman

Astrophil Press
at University of South Dakota
2021

Copyright © 2021 by Vincent James, Rowland Saifi, McCormick Templeman

Layout and design by duncan b. barlow
Additional proofreading provided by Patricia DiMond

Astrophil Press at University of South Dakota
1st pressing 2021

Library of Congress Cataloging-in-Publication Data
Swerve/VINCENT JAMES, ROWLAND SAIFI, MCCORMICK TEMPLEMAN
p. cm.
  ISBN 978-0-9980199-4-9 (pbk. : paper)
  1.Fiction, American
Library of Congress Control Number: 2020945375

http://www.astrophilpress.com

For Z,
- Vincent

For J.G. and T.D.
- Rowland

For Isak Sjursen, the grumpiest saint.
- McCormick

SWERVE ONE

I

It's SUNDAY NIGHT WHEN THELMA CALLS. The Tower needs me in Philadelphia. A new case. They want me to head out tonight. Trouble is, out on the deck of my vacation rental I have a woman in a dress the color and shape of a spring tulip. She's looking for her sister, Fauve. I'm not sure what to make of her. Says this sister went missing or not missing, or might go missing at some point in the very near future. I tell Thelma to tell the higher-ups at The Tower that I'm in the middle of something too big to drop, but I'll take the train to Philly as soon as I'm finished here. Then I head back out and hand a beer to the tulip-dress girl.

Libations, she says, and we clink bottles.

You know, I say, if you look into the sunset at just the right moment, you'll see a green flash. Try it, I say. Her pupils, fixed and dilated, traverse the curves of a mountain descending to slope, masculine lines slipping quick-fingered over chaparral-smoked foothills. She shifts to see what I mean, but finds only thick shrubs and a tree-lined vista extending into the horizon. To the right, I say, and out toward the sea.

Beacons incandesce in the unflagging glimmer of Low-fi summer.

None of it is true, of course, but it gets me thinking, reminding me of a time when there really was an ocean there. When the sea, composed and purple, was a thing expecting to proceed unobstructed.

Green flashes? says the woman, her spider lashes fanning out from irises circumscribed by limbal gloom. What, she wants to know, does any of this have to do with her missing sister? She lights her cigarette and glares—a clean, steady kind of glare, like a cat's tail flicking in anger.

The phone rings again and I know it's Thelma calling me back. I let it go on ringing and focus my attention on my guest. Would you believe me, I say, if I told you this isn't the first I've heard of your sister? When she shakes her head no, I ask her if she's ever met The Woman of the Spring. Negative again. I light another cigarette.

You see, I say, The Woman of the Spring named her daughters after water: Aquifer, Bayou, Caspia, and Po. She'd gathered them up in early infancy from women who'd never meant to have them, these bright tufts of seafoam brought forth on an eager tide. And this was a long time ago, you gotta remember, when a woman's only other option was the nuns up on the hill with their baroque wimples and their sobriquets. (The Woman of the Spring did not care for the nuns on the hill, as one might presume.)

So the young mothers came to The Woman of the Spring, and they left their babes swaddled and mewling. Girls only, she'd requested, but a person would need a very hard heart indeed to turn away a helpless child because he didn't look right in a mermaid suit.

That's how they got Dale and Guy and Peter. There were two others as well, but their mothers came and collected them back one day. The Woman of the Spring didn't like to discuss that, though, and the girls knew better than to mention it. The same thing happened with little Shellby and Monsoon, the youngest, and most gifted of the mermaid sisters. The day Shellby left was the day The Woman of the Spring closed her doors. No new children. No new mermaids. The great red-blue spring of her heart had clamped shut. Valve sealed. Closed for business.

Danube was the new girl. Of course her name wasn't Danube at first. It was something else, something like Amy or Cecily or Jane. She wore a lilac dress that day when she sat in the parlor, the mermaid girls circling her like lions. They'd found her in there, and curious, they'd gone to inspect. Why are you here? demanded Aquifer who, at eighteen, was the oldest and most imperious. But Danube said nothing, only clenched her hands tightly together. Are you feeling shy? asked Caspia, the most beautiful of the mermaids who suffered from secret intractable ailments.

But still Danube did not speak.

I think she doesn't know how, said Po who was secretly thinking about how pretty the girl's lips were and how much she would like to kiss them. And really she was hoping that this mystery girl wouldn't be inducted into the family because, with that figure and those lips, things might prove awkward.

Bayou said nothing. Her heart wasn't in the lion-stalking, and she only followed her sisters' practiced moves, the earthly version of the underwater ring they made each night in their review: *The Madri-Gals Underwater Extravaganza! See 'em before they swim away!* Bayou was thinking about how Po had told her she'd seen something in town the other day. Something she couldn't explain. It had to do with Aquifer.

No more mermaids! shouts Tulip-dress, interrupting my story before it can even get going. I'm tired of hearing about mermaids! It's time for you to listen to my story. She leans back in her deck chair and gazes out toward the eucalyptus trees that line the far edge of the property. Stubbing out her cigarette on the wooden railing, she flicks her chin toward that arboreal militia. Is there someone out there? Out there moving through the trees?

Oh yes. There often is. If she'd let me finish, she'd see how her sister figures in, but she's no longer interested.

She taps her foot lightly against the wood of the deck and begins her tale. Once there was a king and a queen. They were very much in love. Every day he would fetch her special bark from the woods, shaved into paper-fine strips of reddish-brown which he would decoct with cinnamon and dried orange peels for her tea. It was the only thing she desired, and he made sure she had it no matter the weather.

She stops and looks up at me, then flinches at the sound of a bird's call somewhere out in the trees. It's getting on night, she says, and I have to remind her about her story. Where did I leave off? she asks, twisting her cigarette so the cherry light expands and blooms, then dies away.

Around us, dusk sweeps in.

One day, she said, when the king was preoccupied with a rising war in the east, the bark slipped his mind. And that night, when he went to visit his lady in her chambers, when he held her close, when he kissed her lips, when he lifted her skirts, do you know what he found?

I shake my head, and keep my eye trained on those trees all lined up like soldiers. Movement, she says. Torsion. Millions of spindly little legs. And as he tore the garments aside, he found that was all she was: swollen sickness and infiltration. Bot flies and worms. That's all she was. She was never anything else.

I don't understand, I say, and she looks at me like I'm an idiot. Don't you see? She tilts her head. Don't you see? She was never anything else. Under all that silk and tulle, beneath the artifice, there was only ever rot. There was only ever decay. He'd kept it at bay all those years with the cinnamon bark because he didn't want to see. He'd covered it up with baubles and jewels, but one slip, one distraction, one little old war to the east, and the truth reared up and kicked him in the face.

She exhales a wobbly ring of smoke. Beneath it all, she says, sometimes there's nothing but worms.

I shake my head. I'm sorry, but does this story have a point?

It has a point, she says. The point is find my fucking sister.

II

I'M STILL OUTSIDE WITH THE SPIDER-LASHED TULIP woman when the phone rings. Thelma again. It's time to go. I leave Tulip-dress sitting on the deck and head to a bar at the center of town.

Inside the bar, a dog's footprints constellate the dusty floor, but there is no dog in sight. My contact sits on a stool nursing a Guiness. His name is Ermine like the fur, or the animal from which it sprouts. He has with him a leather-bound case, the kind that should contain money, but which instead holds a number of silver bells.

This wasn't what we agreed upon, these bells, but I'm concerned that if I point that out, I will offend him, and Ermine is not the kind of man one wants to offend. Contrarily, a conglomeration of tumescent muscles writhing beneath a cotton tee shirt in vaguely rodent-shaped formations, he is the type of man one wants on one's side or, at the very least, absent from the scene.

Thelma said you needed one of these, he says. Which would you like? Which prosthesis?

I nod along trying to quickly sketch out a hypothesis of this presumed nomenclature. Prosthesis, yes, I think, my mind forming a quick, though admittedly tenuous link from the Greek *pros* and *tithenal*: adding and placing, respectively, through to the idea of the bell which, perhaps (pictographically) one could imagine as a kind of lengthening of the arm through which one might eventually attain the potential to reach the divine. I sip my whiskey and nod, the philological connection fading almost as quickly as it formed.

When I ask about price, he shakes his head. On the house.

I find myself curiously drawn to the bell in the exact center of the case. Its aura is distinctly divergent, possessing a pinkness that I can only describe as primordial. When I reach out to touch it, Ermine flinches. The tendons in his arm extend and contract, slipping willy-nilly up toward those undulating biceps.

The mark is in SF, says Ermine. You're to meet him at Café Trieste. That's where you'll do the hand-off. No later than Saturday.

I nod. I have business in Philly, but I can get to SF by Saturday no problem, I say. He trusts me already. Thinks I'm a lawyer. Thinks I'm his friend.

Ermine nods and slams the case shut before I can touch any more of the bells.

III

THELMA GETS ME A BUSINESS CLASS TRAIN TICKET to Philly and I arrive mid-morning in a daze. The Tower has business for me there, and when the Tower says jump, I say go fuck yourselves. Then I do whatever they ask because they're the Tower. Usually I only work one case at a time, but right now I'm staring down the barrel of three. I've got the Tower gig in Philly, the Café Trieste job in San Fran, and now the freelance number finding Tulip-dress's sister. I'm a sucker for doe eyes and a sob story. After this batch I'm going to need a vacation.

As I exit the train, I notice I've spilled some mystery liquid all down the front of my shirt, and though I don't remember doing it, I do remember the family across the aisle from me giving me odd looks, a parent's protective arm shooting out to stop a little one from approaching me.

In the station, a gaggle of kids in black knit bonnets sits lined up on a bench. I stop to talk to one of them, but when he opens his mouth to speak, it forms a little circle, and the words come out in an impossible hiss. The girl beside him puts a hand on his knee and looking up at me, she shakes her head.

That's not a good idea, she says, and then with a flick of her wrist in the direction of the exit sign, she says run along now. That's a good boy.

I notice she has a beauty mark in the shape of a heart at the center of her palm. Beside it, a finely demarcated X. Overcome by a strange compulsion like a chorus of whispering angels pulling me onward, I nearly reach out to touch that X. But then a woman in a wimple arrives and gives me a look.

I'm sorry, I say, taking a step away from the child. Are they your students? Are they orphans?

The woman glares at me and the light changes, cloud cover shifting through the train station windows, and in this new light, I see that she is no more wearing a wimple than I am, but rather a ruffled white turtleneck. When I look back there are only two children, neither of whom wears a bonnet. The whispering boy plays with a hand-held game system, and the girl wears a shirt depicting an anthropomorphic waterfall wearing sunglasses. *Too Cool*, the waterfall says. The girl grins big enough that I see her incisors, and then calmly, coolly, she gives me the middle finger.

On Market Street, I dip into an alley, taking the back way to the apartment in question. An old school chum of someone high up at the Tower has gone missing.

Halfway down a side alley, I locate the back door. It's ajar. I climb three dimly-lit flights of concrete steps up to the apartment, which I find unlocked. Inside, there is no furniture. Only books stacked throughout the living room in neat rows like biblio-skyscrapers. When I step into the room, I notice that the wood is slick, a thin layer of water flowing between the books. A kind of Venice. I walk the linoleum canals, touching the top of a stack now and then. The presence of such an astounding quantity of expertly arranged books intrigues me. In the kitchen, I notice that the cupboards are bare. In the bathroom there is neither toilet paper, nor medicine in the cabinet, though the dossier paints him as an enthusiastic, if ill-considering taker of both the benzodiazepines and the opioids.

In the closet hangs a piece of notepaper stuck through with the curved tip of a metal hanger. It reads:

DG: Went West.

After unhooking the note, I make my way back to the living room and stare at the rows of books. Starting at the near end I count four rows down (D being the fourth letter in the alphabet), and seven over (G being the seventh). I run a finger down along the spines of the books in the pile until I locate Nathaniel West's *The Day of The Locust*. When I pull it from the stack and flip it open to the first page, I find a torn photograph. Taken at some kind of aquatic amusement park, it's a grainy snap of a bride and groom. On the back, in loopy pencil is written: Sal Giancana and Aquifer? Taken 1954?

I slip it into my pocket and make my way out of the apartment, and down the cracked and tilted tenement steps. Outside, I see a figure rounding the corner at the end of the alley.

Intent on following, I start down the alley but soon find myself distracted by a particularly spindly-legged spider. Determining him, perhaps ill-advisedly, to be a possible informant, I pace him as he skitters up over a drain pipe and then back down again, along the pock-marked wall and around a corner I'd not realized was a corner (due to an optical illusion, which I ought to describe in great detail at some later point), and into another, even smaller alley into which, because of my broad shoulders, I can only fit if I turned to my side. Deep into that crevasse, I kick-ball-change after Marvin the spider, whose name I, by this point, have intuited, until he comes to rest at the center of a graffiti symbol that in the darkness looks almost like blood spatter. I take out my phone and am trying to encourage it to act like a flashlight when I remember that the thing no longer works in most capacities, and hasn't since an unfortunate incident concerning a violently amorous squirrel and an uncovered pool in winter.

Fishing in my back pocket I locate the flashlight I keep for just such emergencies, and when I shine it on the symbol, I see a spiraling flower design drawn as if by a small child. In its center is written: for-keeps. After thanking Marvin for the hot tip, I squeeze myself back out onto the main alleyway only to find the man I've been following is now waiting for me. He stands with his arms out to the side as if waiting to be struck down by some act of God. When nothing happens, he looks at me with curiosity.

Up close, I see he wears a bent clerical collar, overly worn and grayish from careless washing. He's holding a coffee cup with lipstick marks around the rim.

Aquifer left, you know, says the priest. Left in the middle of the night. I'll be looking out West, he says. Taking the Greyhound. When he turns to go, I notice a long white thread trailing behind him. Upon closer inspection, I see it's a line of albino fire ants.

I call Thelma and tell her I'll be taking the bus instead of the train out to SF. I've got a priest to follow. The next morning, after eating a ham sandwich slopped with mayonnaise thick as glue, I buy a ticket and board the bus, careful to position myself some distance away from the priest. Beside me sits a man in a silver hat and Dickey's coveralls. He eats Slim Jims slowly, but with great alacrity. I think about asking him if I can have one, but instead I busy myself with a game of mental solitaire (I never let myself win), and stare out the window at the passing clouds, the sinking sun, the reds, the greens, the fields blipping past like rows of shotgun shells.

Exactly when we reach the halfway point of our journey, the man in the silver hat leans over and whispers: There are people watching you.

I know, I reply.

He nods and takes a bite of a Slim Jim. He says, I know about the Woman of the Spring too.

This surprises me so I pull out a notepad and pen. He extends his hand and I shake it. Name's Ros, he tells me. He sucks on his Slim Jim for a while and then nods, finally ready to begin.

I found her down among the rocks and the cedars, he says, his voice growing deeper, more resonant, almost like he's channeling some unseen orator. I found the curve of her breast illuminated by a swollen, thankless moon. No ordinary woman, she told me things that would come to pass and I believed her. She told me her astral secrets and of the way that time whispers through the trees. I forgot her until just the other day.

He offers me a Slim Jim, and I take it. He nods and taps his silver hat with his ring finger.

One night, he says, she took me out beyond the city limits, over to where the animals no longer live, and she showed me the lip of a cave. Reaching up to touch it, I felt something there in the moss-lined furrow of its aperture. Upon further examination, I discovered that it was a brass key, its bow embellished with fleur-de-lis. Immediately I recognized it as belonging to the great wooden door that opened onto my childhood bedroom, or rather, the antechamber to my childhood bedroom in which my mother had created a child's sitting room in which no children ever sat. There was a sky blue couch, adorned with a hexagonal throw pillow and a cross-hatched blanket made by some distant aunt. And there was a curio cabinet painted the color of lilacs when they die. On one shelf in particular, she'd placed what in retrospect must have been the physical manifestations of her hopes and dreams for me. On that shelf there was a painting of a man, a watercolor impression of a slim man in a dark suit walking down a boulevard I can only assume must have been in Paris. This is the person she hoped I'd become.

I take a bite of the meat stick and nod. Your mom, I ask, did she ever mention this Woman of the Spring?

The man shakes his head. No, he says, never. But in her sitting room, she had a similar display case. A glass cabinet filled with gifts my father had given her whenever he'd returned, bilious and guilt-ridden from some foreign locale. Ivory predominated. Carved into intricate patterns, the ivory pieces stood in military formation, their line never breaking. One piece, I remember, took the shape of an egg, its shell carved into lacey filigree, the workmanship of which was next to astounding, and inside, where the yoke ought to have been, stood a solitary elephant, its trunk raised hopefully, triumphantly. Even then, before I understood the necessary diabolism of its acquisition, I knew somehow that the elephant stood as a prescient reminder of what would eventually come to pass.

What did you do with the key? I ask Ros. I gave it to you, he says, and then looks away. Then where is it? I ask, but he shakes his head. He's sucking on his Slim Jim like he's being paid to do it.

A few seats up, the Priest is listening to a Walkman from the 1980s with orange spongey headphones. Sometimes I think he's not a priest at all. Sometimes I think his face changes with each passing stop.

IV

IN NEW MEXICO I FIND THELMA. You're in trouble, she says. Too much mixing of sundry and psychotropic substances, not enough doing your actual damn job. If the Tower wants me to do my job, I tell her, they can book me a plane, but she just gives me a look.

We both know I'm not allowed to fly anymore.

I met Thelma several years ago when I came-to quite abruptly, mid-coitus. There she'd appeared, a halo of motel room lamp-glow encircling her bouffant, her nipples ringed with what at first glance I'd thought must be tiny blue octopi. Later I'd realize they were just pasties she'd neglected to remove after her shift at Slippy McGovern's House of Coot, an establishment where, she explained, I'd been lucky enough to make her acquaintance.

Since that day in the motel room, it's been me and Thelma all the way.

I'm the one who got Thelma mixed up with the Tower. Now she acts as my go-between, procuring my assignments, researching my cases, and generally protecting my interests. Thelma has a name that makes me think of the thalamus and the thymus, which a girl I once dated told me shrivels inside us as we age. She used to rub her breastbone and say, ooh, my thymus gland sure hurts today. Eventually she went crazy. Got pregnant from some guy I didn't know and moved to Austrolasia to study Blue-rings.

Blueheelers? Thelma asks and I realize I must have been thinking aloud about my thymus girl and her psychological breakdown or ecological breakthrough. We're back in our motel again. Our usual spot for debriefing. It's only Wednesday. Plenty of time still until Saturday, so we're lounging in bed, my arm slipped around her shoulder, her apple-scented head soft upon my chest. I'm showing her the photo I found in Philadelphia.

Not Blueheelers, I say. Blue-rings. Blue-ringed Octopi.

Octopuses, she corrects. I just love octopuses.

She wouldn't like these, I suspect. Very few people do.

You're supposed to be in San Francisco meeting your mark, she says, so what are you doing freelancing in New Mexico? I tell her I have a suspicion about this priest I'm following, but more than that, I've got a pain in my heart that told me I couldn't pass up a chance to swing by Slippy McGovern's and see my best gal. She thinks I'm joking, but I'm being sincere. I really do have a terrible pain in my heart.

Do you know what pain is? she asks. What it really is? It's a chemical reaction. She lights a cigarette. Nociceptors, sensory neurons that shuttle these messages right on up to like, the thalamus, which hands them out to wherever they're supposed to go. Most of mine go to the amygdala, she says. I suspect because of, you know, emotions.

I think about asking her why she always knows stuff like that, but then I remember about thymus girl and discover I probably have some sexual predilection for left brain dominant women—something I hope to fashion into a genuine paraphilia someday if I can muster the energy, which I probably can't.

Later, when Thelma and I are on our way to a donut shop, we find the priest. He's washing a car in a driveway, pretending to be the father of four in his buttoned down shirt and penny loafers. That night we see him by the side of the highway, a teenage girl in a hooded sweatshirt just trying not to be seen. The next morning he's a woman with a dog that openly dislikes me. He's a man with a tattered yellow raincoat that tells me he's got six more where that came from. He's a procession of modern day saints lurching toward Slippy McGovern's. He's a pill in a bottle dissolved until it's a solution.

There is no solution Thelma says. We're back in the motel room and I'm off the topic, off the case, off my tits on speed and poppers (of all things), off the bed now and onto the floor where I puddle.

There's always a solution she says again.

I nod, though my head feels like it's filled with ball bearings, and I fall asleep on the floor. In my dreams, I sink my teeth into the flesh of a particularly sweet ewe. I come away with blood dripping down my chin, pooling on the dirt beneath me. In the waking world, Thelma sighs deeply.

When I wake again, Thelma is gone. The bed is neatly made. Hospital corners. For the first time I notice there are blood stains on the wall. Not fresh, thank god. Old arterial spray with a vaguely Rorschachian feel to it. I see an octopus dress floating in a silver forest. I see an astronaut lost in his own orbit. I see a lardass detective who probably needs to lay off the poppers.

On the bed where Thelma used to be is a zine. It's old, black and white. Photocopied. I can't make out the image on the cover, but there's a date and location. PDX 1995. Inside is written a single line:

Under the dust of a city that once was, I take what is mine.

V

1995

Under the dust of a city that once was, I take what is mine.

I pull on my pants, fold up the zine, and slip it into my pocket, before making my way outside into the violent glare of mid-day. Across the highway there's a sun-bleached billboard for a water park. A mermaid show every night at 8:00 PM. *The Madri-Gals Underwater Extravaganza! See 'em before they swim away!* I shake my head and laugh. When my gaze lands on two RV's parked side-by-side across the road, I suspect it is time for a cigarette. The sun is positioned at a curious angle, and beneath that strange and pregnant sun, I begin to wonder about the time. I look down at my wrist but find it naked.

If you want to know if you're dreaming, I remember Thelma saying once, find a digital clock. Look at the numbers and then quickly look away. When you look back again, if you're dreaming, the numbers will change. They will always be different. Not so in real life. That's how you can tell who you really are.

I stare out at the RV's. I think I see movement out in one, but I can't be sure. I take out the zine and start reading.
Under the dust of a city that once was, I take what is mine.

I'm seeing a show at La Luna, and the sound system is turned up too loud and there is feedback and the gin and tonics are too weak, and the mosh-pit is too filled with elbows. I've already had one visit to the dentist thanks to an overly enthusiastic plaid-clad knee to the jaw, and I don't need another. There's a girl there in a black and white daisy dress. Staring at me. A silver bracelet snakes all the way up her arm.

Blips of time condense and expand. The feedback reaches an apotheosis in a screech of Erinyeic proportions, and then the girl is standing beside me.

"I like your shirt," she says, and when I look down I see that I no longer wear the tattered Cure shirt I'd put on before leaving my apartment on Belmont, and am instead wearing something low-cut and lacy with flowers all over it.

"This isn't my shirt," I tell her.

"Sometimes," the girl says, "do you feel like the male gaze is too intrusive? That it changes things around us as we go? That it starts to shape our reality? Because I do. My name's Annuli, by the way." She holds out her hand and I shake it.

"I'm sorry, but do I know you?"

"We have friends in common," she says. "Or we will have in the future if we don't now."

She extends her snake bracelet arm and brazenly drops something into my drink. Like, she doesn't even try to conceal it. She just does it.

"Did you just roofie me?"

"No," she says. "I slipped you a mickey. There's a difference."

I shake my head. This is always happening in Portland.

"I'm not going to drink it."

"Sure you are," she says with a wink.

She puts her arm around my shoulder and points up at the black ceiling. "Do you ever wonder if none of this is real? Like maybe we're not even here? Like maybe we're somewhere else, somewhere hot and dry and, I don't know, pornographic, and we're just like being, you know, watched."

I shrug and take a sip of my drink.

"I don't know either," she says. "But I have my suspicions. Like, time, right? It's so much like light. Like, light's all, ooh, look at me. I'm a particle; but now look—I'm also a wave! We get it already." She shrugs and stares into my eyes. "Time's exactly the same way."

Things are slipping in and out of my vision.

"Who are you?" I slur.

"I told you. My name is Fauve."

"No, you said it was something different before."

"Would you look at that shirt of yours?"

I look down and see it's almost my shirt—same color, same holes from wear— but now it's a Smiths shirt.

"I don't even like the Smiths" I say.

She raises an eyebrow. "It's that male gaze again. Sometimes the male gets sloppy with his gaze. He drinks too much and he does poppers (of all things), and he stands out in the sun looking at those RV's for too long and then he can't hold the fabric together anymore. He lets it slip. Do you see what I mean?"

I squint at her, thinking maybe I do know her from somewhere.

"You said your name is Fauve, right?"

She stares back at me, her expression blank.

"Who's Fauve?"

Later that night I ditch the guy I've been seeing and I walk home alone. I just want some goddamned sleep, but at three in the morning, I wake up to the sound of someone throwing rocks at my window. Outside, leaning against the streetlamp that for some reason is emitting a red glow, my best friend, Isak, is three sheets to the wind. The red light glints off the metal studs on his leather jacket.

When I let him in, he's beside himself. He's made a mistake, he says. He borrowed Amy's car, and well, here's the thing, he says, sheepish in that belligerent way of his, He's kind of lost it.

"But Isak," I say, "you don't have a license. You don't drive."

"Tell that to the car," he says, and then he asks me if we have any beer, and my housemates do. It's Weinhard's of course. I can't drink beer, though I like how the brewery on the hill smells like alphabet soup and when it closes down some years from now, I'll never feel the same way about the city, like all my love and hope and yearning were all contained for better or worse in that alphabet soup stink.

I get my keys and we drive around the city, me struggling to keep my eyes open and Isak muttering about how maybe he should just move back to Chicago.

When we find Amy's car, the tires are missing. We stand in front of it and Isak nods wisely like this makes total sense to him.

We go to the Hotcake House.

Mid-hotcake, the girl appears again. Her name is Djuna now, not Fauve, and she introduces herself to me as a geneticist. Isak seems to know her from somewhere and keeps looking at me as if to ask: I didn't sleep with her, did I?

Djuna invites us to a party even though it's four in the morning by this point, but I think what the hell?

The party is filled with people I don't know and people I vaguely recognize—like a girl who works at Sassy's, a strip joint where a friend of mine also works and on slow nights this friend asks me to come and put dollar bills down in front of her when she dances—her own money—to model the behavior for the asshole customers who never pony up. Good job! I try to say with my eyes. Thumbs up! Your vagina is looking fantastic!

The girl at the party who works at Sassy's asks me where the bathroom is, and I tell her I have no idea. The guy I'm supposed to be hooking up with is there too. He gives me sad eyes from across the room, and I wave like we're just friends or like I know him vaguely from that one time at the DMV and then I duck into the kitchen. Djuna or Fauve is standing there alone. She reaches out her hand and touches my cheek.

"I have to tell you something," she says, "it's bad."

There's more, but I'm not ready to read it, so I close the zine. When I look up, the RV's are gone, only empty horizon left in their wake. I drop my cigarette and stub it out with the heel of my boot. Reaching in my back pocket, I find a set of car keys. I don't remember renting a car. I wonder if Thelma lent me hers.

I don't check out of the motel because, let's face it, this isn't going to end well for anyone. I locate the car which is so covered in such deeply personalized detritus that I wonder if I haven't actually owned this car for years, decades even maybe.

I have to get to San Francisco. To Café Trieste. I tuck a bird of paradise into my lapel.

I get in the car and start driving.

SWERVE TWO

I

YES, I SAID, KNOWING THAT I WOULD. I'd been somewhat shiftless, between projects and at loose ends, when I decided to go to the meeting at Caffe Trieste in North Beach. I saw the Bird of Paradise sitting at the corner table where I liked to sit and look busy during the week. It was the moody table, I liked to call it. I was going to call you, but, the lawyer said, and waved his hands about like the seagulls at Sutro Baths, and then suddenly dropped them in his lap. Two birds, one stone. The coffee is yours, he said.

I felt the cup, and it was still warm.

Thank you, I said and took a sip. There was something seductive about the Bird of Paradise in his lapel.

So, before I go into all of this, I wanted to ask: what do you do when you aren't doing this? I mean, Thelma said you aren't a full-time detective, the lawyer said.

I mentioned that I was going to give a short talk at a gallery on Geary in July. The man with the flower had an iced tea. I didn't know what a Bird of Paradise looked like until then, and it didn't seem like a flower one would wear in a lapel. I had to stop myself from staring.

Where on Geary? the lawyer said.

Geary and Hyde, I said.

That's not a gallery, he said.

Then he proceeded to tell me about the job: a missing persons case. He needed help locating someone for yet another client. I wasn't really a P.I. although I'd gotten a license some years before in a moment of crisis—feeling like what I had been doing up until then had no relevance in the world and wanting to do something with tangible results, I took a few criminal justice classes and applied. The only time I inhabited my crisis-career was when I took cases for my friend Thelma, it mostly involved background checks and the like. Sometimes I'd get to do what I called field work, but I had a bad habit of letting some small detail capture my attention more than what I was there to do. Like when I was tailing a slip-and-fall case and ended up with a year of swing dance lessons or when following a cheating spouse, I'd gotten lost at the Exploratorium only to come-to in a panic in the middle of some exhibit, the subject nowhere in sight. My camera was mostly full of pictures of the exhibits and their descriptions that I'd started taking for a cover but soon started taking for myself. After a few times of this happening, Thelma decided that I should be given a flat fee whenever I went out in the field, as I called it. And so recently I've started declining her jobs. This was different, however, because she's never referred me to anyone before, and I couldn't tell if this was a sign of confidence or a gentle breaking of our relationship.

I felt from the first moment I heard about you that you'd be perfect for the job, the flower man said, all you have to do is go and dig around, and if you don't come up with anything, at least you get to take a small vacation.

And if you do find something, follow it, the lawyer added, but to tell you the truth, it's better for everyone if we don't find out where the target is, really, I just need to show our client that I hired someone to look for him. And the more time you spend on the case, the more it looks like I did the due diligence and can get onto other aspects of this case. Even if you don't find the target, it's still billable for you, your friend, and ourselves, so like I said: you'd be perfect for the job.

I tried to make a mental note to ask Thelma what she had said about me. The man took a contract out of his briefcase and pushed it towards me. You'll notice, it's not a flat fee like you are used to and I hope that's not a problem—you'll be billing each hour. Plus, you can put all expenses on this, he said, waving an expensive looking black credit card at me before setting it down on the paperwork followed by an expensive looking fountain pen. I can tell you need the money. So, take the opportunity to go get lost and have a vacation down south in wine country. Just send me an update now and then so that I can pass them on to my client. Deal?

I thought Napa was north of here, I said.

There's more than one wine country, the flower man said, It boils down to this: I don't care where you wind up, really, but you have to at least step foot in Ojai.

Why is that, I said.

Just go there, and then, as long as you can justify it, go wherever you like, that's all our client asks. Just make it convincing enough for the client, or whoever else might poke around.

I nodded, signed the paper, then said, The coldest winter is June in San Francisco.

Sure, the flower man said. Listen do you want anything else? Sandwich, cookie? Maybe a salad?

No, I said, The coffee was good, thank you.

Ok, but, why pass up a free meal?

You'll need one—you should leave ASAP, the lawyer said. In fact, it would be best case scenario if you leave when you're done with your sandwich. He snatched the paper from me and put it back in his briefcase.

I'm good.

Listen, you need to start thinking: billable. He ordered a sandwich, then paid, and left before it arrived. I realized that I was still holding the pen, and after examining the gold nib which was etched with lovely Deco details, I inadvertently squirted a blob of violet ink on the tabletop just in time to be witnessed by the barista setting down the sandwich. My inky fingers stained the escaping mayonnaise purple.

Despite living in California for nearly a decade, I'd never been down the 101. I found no reason to leave San Francisco much less move out of my Tenderloin apartment. After college I fell into a job at an ice cream shop in the Upper Fillmore. Soon I was in a rhythm of doling out ice cream for eight hours and doing my other work for as long as it needed. While ice cream wasn't a delightful career, I enjoyed the job because I didn't really need to think about anything but my other work. The ease of the job along with the weight of the books I'd lined the walls, floors, window seat, and tables of my small pair of rooms have, over the years, come to preclude any thoughts of leaving my little warren. Emperor Norton never left his, why would I? The volumes had bricked me in. Even that day, after leaving the café, the majority of my time was spent selecting books to take with me. Once

I'd settled on *A History of The Voice; The Gold Bug and Other Tales;* and *Toothpaste, a Romance,* everything else was easy to pack. I put my camera, a notebook, the recently-acquired fountain pen, three pencils, and my pair of binoculars, in a small satchel and dressed in what I call my Everyday Joe clothes: a pair of tan chinos, a sea green knit shirt, and a red windbreaker, all topped with a white ball cap that read, *Shrimp and Grits,* which I wear when tailing people. But should I bring shorts? Was it really that much warmer down south as I had imagined? I didn't know. I didn't own shorts. By the time I decided I could buy shorts once I got there, if the weather warranted it, the only car I could get at the rental place was a red muscle car with Florida plates that smelled like orange soda with an undercurrent of rotten milk (it might have been me) that I decided to call it Torito. Still, after breaking free of the city, I felt a relief that I hadn't expected, and as my speed increased, so did the volume of Torito's radio.

II

IT WAS DINNERTIME WHEN I GOT TO SANTA BARBARA, and I settled on a less attractive diner called Craven' Dish. The letters in the sign were flickering. Strangely, there were only four other people there: a couple, one with dark hair and glasses, the other blond with glasses who looked to be tired; there was a man with striking red hair and a beard, his ears full of piercings, who was scrawling in a notebook and drinking a chocolate shake; and the fourth seemed to be asleep, his head on a place-mat and surrounded by crayons. I wasn't sure where to begin, except to eat meatloaf and drink generic black tea, labeled simply *tea*. There was something elegant in that, I thought. I took out my notebook and recorded the day's driving, making a special note of the patch of rosemary by the water and a clump of seals I happened to disturb while looking for a suitable place to urinate. Then, I drew a small diagram of the case so far: a triangle with three points and a line down the center, but I was unable yet to label the diagram. I ate and looked out at Torito, backlit by the sunset in the lot. I couldn't see the ocean just beyond the parking lot but could smell it. It was all around me and even though it was a little warmer, the breeze from the water compensated. Ojai was still a little way away, and I closed my eyes to imagine what it would look like, what I would do there, and finally, imagined that I would find who I was looking for sunning himself on a beach. That we had both failed to find who we were looking for—he, his missing person, and me, my missing person—although, I guess, if I was there with him, he would be the only one who had not found anyone. But then I thought, why had I imagined that he was looking for anyone? Why had I imagined that indeed he had found his missing person, and he and I, and his missing person, were all on the beach together enjoying the sun, satisfied with a job well done. I decided that I would send a postcard, *from the blazing beaches of Ojai,* when I got there.

Hey, you awake? The waitress prodded me with her pen. You want dessert or just the check?

I was just lost in thought.

You and that guy, she pointed to the man with his head down.

I'm sorry, is he okay?

Him? No. He's a scientist, if you'd believe it. Works up at the Towers.

The Towers?

Las Cumbres Observatory. We call it the Towers around here. We call him The Guardian of the Dark Towers. The man lifted his head, rubbed his face, and waved over to the waitress. Excuse me, she said, the darkness is beckoning.

I watched her walk over and stand there while the man patted and dug around in every pocket he had as well as between the seat cushions of the booth. The waitress was about to call the cook over, who it seemed also acted as a bouncer, when I got up and, with the mantra, *billable* in my head, I went over to his table and asked for his bill to be added to mine. Are you sure about that, the waitress said.

Billable, I said.

The man seemed to be sitting as still as he could, as if about to frighten a deer or rabbit.

The waitress looked at him, then me, squinting a little, and said, Well, that's real big of you. I'll write up a new bill.

I like to tip well, the man said.

When he bothers to pay, she said.

Well, at least this one is on me, I said feeling a little unsure of my decision, it's part of my job.

Oh, reality TV, huh? the waitress asked.

I smiled, tapping my nose.

The bathroom's out of order, she said and walked away.

The man smiled and thanked me. He introduced himself as Dr. Clinnemann. I shook his hand and told him my name. He said, listen, are you going to be around for a while? I need to run back to my office and get my wallet, so I can pay you back.

No problem, I said, I have an expense account. It's not my money anyway. All I ask, to make it legit, is that you tell me if you have seen anyone who looks like this? I showed him the picture the man had given me for just this purpose.

Are you serious? he asked.

Yeah, that way it's an expense, I said.

Well, what am I supposed to say?

I don't know, just, have you seen him?

I've seen him, but I don't know him. But I'm getting the sense he might be a little bit of a creep, maybe a little off he said.

He works in reality television, the waitress said, setting down the receipt.

Oh, he said, How do you want me to answer? How about this: I've, never seen him until just now. He laughed.

Ok, I said, job done and expense justified. Then went back over to wait for my food, which was delivered without comment.

Hey, he got up and walked over to my booth, if you won't let me pay you back, at least let me give you a tour of the observatory. It might be good for your show, and it would get us some publicity.

As long as you let me eat my waffles first, I said, I'd be happy to. But I'm not sure it will be good publicity.

Any publicity is good publicity, isn't that what they say? And if it comes by way of some weird show, then so be it, he said and handed me his card. The address is my office, just come when you are done here. And with that, he left.

For some reason, it seemed, everyone was a little cool to me after that. I had to walk up to the register just to get the bill, which it turned out, was nearly three hundred dollars. I said to myself, *billable*, and wrote in a seventy-dollar tip. I paused to admire the violet ink drying slowly on the receipt.

The drive up to the Towers was confusing, and Torito grumbled and hesitated at the small winding hills up to the observatory. I patted his dash. Like most of his generation, it seemed that Torito had opted for weight over reps, and while his red frame displayed an impressive bulk that was able to leap up short, steep hills, almost to the point of being airborne, he struggled to traverse a steady incline. I soon found myself coming upon an array of domes, one of which, it seemed, had its mouth hanging open and tongue sticking out. Dr. Clinnemann's office was in the basement, and there was a note for me on the dry erase board: *waiting for you in the planetarium,* and below a bare-bones map. I found the door and walked into the room. It was much like a large theater and nearly completely dark. Take a seat, Dr. Clinnemann said through a PA system hidden somewhere in the darkness. I'd sit somewhere in the middle—I mean, you've got the whole place to yourself.

I did as he suggested and discovered that the seat reclined so that I was staring at the ceiling and immediately found it comforting. The seat rumbled, and there was a great explosion projected above me. This, said a recorded voice in what seemed to be a slightly British accent, is the birth of the universe...Imagine the force, the energy at the edge of creation. The seat rumbled each time an animated flaming and forming planet zoomed by or an asteroid streaked the firmament or whenever a somewhat sentimental star exploded, and I tried to remember the saying that was supposed to help me remember the order of the planets, but I found myself getting lost because I could easily remember the order of the planets but not the mnemonic.

It was while thinking of pizza, mothers, and milk money that I must have drifted to sleep because it seemed as if the projection had zoomed in on one of the small marble-like globes, and I found myself suddenly working as a barber who kept a large cat with grey and black matted fur in a small bag. I spent the day shaving and weighed each customer's beard—some top, some bottom, some both—before handing the customers a receipt with the weight listed in a careful hand. The shop smelled of witch hazel, verbena, and cat litter. At the end of the day. I would put on my rough jacket and carry the bags of hair to a woman named Mauve, who then took the bag of hair and spun it into yarn. While she worked, she told me an old story: Once upon a time, a Rabbit had seven children. She loved her children and would protect them from The Last Wolf. One day, as the sun was getting low in the sky, she said to her children, dear children, I must go out and get us food. So be on guard for The Last Wolf. Pay close attention, because he may disguise himself, but you will always recognize him by his wide feet. If he gets in, he will eat you all. After saying this, she left. No sooner was there a call at the door in the voice of their mother who said, Open up, children I've brought you beautiful things! But the children looked through the crack in the door and said, you aren't our mother, we see your wide feet. Disgruntled, The Last Wolf went into town and bought a pair shoes that made his feet as narrow and sleek as the Rabbit's and went back to the Rabbit's home, and said, children, open the door, I've brought you some beautiful things! But The Last Wolf was too excited by the ruse and smiled a vicious smile, and when the children saw his long teeth through the crack, they said, you're not our mother, she doesn't have long teeth all the way around! Angered, The Last Wolf went back into town and found a dentist and demanded that all but his two front teeth be removed. After his gums were stripped clean but for two gleaming teeth, he went back to the warren and said, children, children, open up. I've run The Last Wolf off and brought you some beautiful things! The children looked through the crack and saw what looked like their mother Rabbit at the door, and opened it. When The Last Wolf entered, they ran to hide—one beneath the bed, one under the sink, one in the wardrobe, one in the broom closet, one behind the couch, one inside a clock, and one behind the curtains, but it was too late. He found and ate all the children but the one hiding in the clock. Having naught but two front teeth, the daggers he called them, he had to swallow each whole, which gave him a terrible stomach ache, and so he decided to go lie down by a riverbank lined with silver. When the mother returned home, she learned of what happened to her children from the child hiding in the clock and ran to the silver riverbank and found The Last Wolf sleeping. She gnawed open belly of The Last Wolf and found each of her children, who having been swallowed whole, were still alive. She bade them to make models of themselves out of the heavy silver clay of the riverbank, and once they had done this, she placed each of these effigies of her children in The Last Wolf's stomach and sewed it back up with thread spun from her own coat. When The Last Wolf woke, he was incredibly thirsty and went to the river to drink. When he drank, the water and silvery mud mixed in his stomach, expanded and spread through his body. The Last Wolf died there, a gleaming statue draped in fur. The mother brought her children back home and kissed each one on their head, all except the seventh one, who had hidden in the clock. My dear little child, she said to the seventh child, instead of helping your siblings, you hid in the clock, and so you will live your life forever under the sign of the clock and only imagine your life outside for eternity. You will hear the lives of your siblings and their children and children's children, you will hear the world free of wolves but never again see them or join in their games. Then, she threw the cursed child into the clock and nailed the door shut.

As the hammer fell upon the clock, I woke to the sound of another explosion and the recorded voice saying, With the universe still in a state of expanding and our technical capabilities severely limited, Astral Projection is the only real way to fully explore the universe. Refined by a Dutch Alchemist, known only as Zilvenaar, in the early part of the 17th century and kept secret by a secret order formed shortly after, Astral Projective Space Travel has had a significant impact on our understanding of the universe. Astral Projection, however, is a difficult skill and requires in some cases, more rigorous training than a standard astronaut. This is because the task of the Astral Projection-aut is the inversion of an Astronaut's. Where the astronaut seeks absolute control, the Projectionaut requires almost total surrender. Instead of a capsule of titanium and porcelain, the Projectionaut has only the flesh they are born into and like the space capsule, it must be kept in perfect shape; but as in traditional space travel, the Projectionaut must also possess a stronger will; without a dead-to-centered self, there is a chance that the Projectionaut may suffer a split between worlds and sometimes an infinite number of worlds and must then find those splintered selves over galaxies and time... Suddenly Clinnemann cut in: Sorry, sorry. That is a joke track we made for our holiday party, he said, it's kind of an insider's thing—there's this group up in the hills, cult really, who believe in this stuff and we thought it might be funny to record something...

Oh, I said into the darkness.

Anyway, if astral projection worked, we'd see it, right? There would be empirical evidence.

Right, I said.

Hold on, he said and was soon standing in the aisle. Want to look through the telescope?

Why not?

We left one building and walked along a path among the towering domes I'd seen while driving up. It was a quiet walk, and the stars stretching out to the sea were shimmering above us. The whole time we didn't encounter another soul. We went inside the dome whose mouth was hanging open, and it looked like how I imagined the inside of a Victorian dam might look. A number of wheels and pipes. A grouping of wooden chairs and a table covered in papers. We walked over to a large instrument with a lens. Here, he said, look through here.

I put my eye to a binocular sort of eye-piece and saw beyond it a hazy milky collection of blazing worlds, dulcet and strangely boring.

Nice, isn't it, he said, entrancing...one of the few here you can actually look through. The rest have different sensory arrays.

Yes, I said, it's beautiful.

And each one a solar system, with planets and who knows, life? Spirits? Some believe that we go to another planet in the end, another reality so much like our own where we live again our same lives.

Life.

Dr. Clinnemann was suddenly a little distant. Well, I mean, if you believe in that. Do you believe, can you believe that people believe that stuff? Like astral projection as a scientific tool for observing these universes?

I don't know. I've always felt that I'll figure it out when I get there and, in the meantime, why bother guessing?

He laughed. Well, I could take you somewhere where we all believe, he said and gripped my shoulders, staring in my eyes. There are others here, and despite what they say, it's real science and we're all working on something new. I mean, no one can understand the new, the revolutionary. Astral projection is a scientific means to examine up close the billions of planets out there. To see which ones are populated, which ones could be populated. To try and contact the other selves that populate those worlds. To travel to the past and the future. It is the only way to travel beyond the speed of light. Dr. Clinnemann seemed to be trembling slightly, That man in the picture you showed me, I think he looks like someone who might believe, who might be uniquely suited for the job.

Is he there, with the cult?

No, but he could be, in some other planet, he might already be a member of our scientific congress.

But he isn't now?

No. But I hope that when he is done with his search, he'll find us. You know where to find us, here at the Towers.

I was feeling a little uneasy. I can't say that I understood what he was talking about, and it seemed that he'd gotten something a little mixed up or was maybe playing me. Well, Dr., I said, Thank you for the show, but I have to check into my hotel room before midnight and I still got a ways to drive. I wish you the best.

He grinned, in a kind of gently condescending way. Ok, he said. Well, know that even if you don't understand it, you are part of this. I'm part of this. He pointed to the telescope. Whatever you see out there, he said, putting his finger to my forehead, you can find it right there. We are all part of this fabric of reality, this amazing intersection of worlds, tilting ever slowly towards a single reality.

I bowed and left him standing in his Victorian dam.

III

THE DRIVE TO OJAI WAS SHORTER THAN I THOUGHT and I was disappointed to find there was no ocean to speak of. It was too late to check in to the Rancho Inn, although there was a note left for me from my employer asking for an update. What I could see of the town at night consisted of a main strip of an arched portico on one side and a large park on the other. I parked in a lot on the backside of the park and, under the warm glow of Torito's dome light, I opened my notebook and tried to update the map I'd drawn earlier and to gather my thoughts for the update I was sure to have to deliver. I looked at the triangle and drew another one inverted at the apex, but I still couldn't label the sides yet, and certainly couldn't place Dr. Clinnemann, however—he seemed to belong in two places on the map. I turned to a new page and simply made a list of people I'd encountered so far and then on each successive page, a cloud of words I felt were associated with each person. It was almost like a short book of poems. When I was done, I curled up and had a restless snooze in Torito's backseat, his embrace sheltering me from the blazing worlds of the night sky.

IV

ONE THING I WAS DISCOVERING ABOUT OJAI WAS that the mornings were quite unlike the foggy dawns of SF. The grass was damp. The sky was clear. The park was beautiful in the warm morning light, and I decided to stroll through it. I thought for a moment that I saw someone I knew, but it turned out to be a vagrant bathing in a water fountain. When I got to the street, I saw beneath one of the arches what looked to be a popular café. Even though the line inside was long, when it was my turn to order, I had trouble deciding what to get, and after a few faltering selections (and a grumpy comment from the woman with green hair behind me), I got an apple turnover and a large coffee. I settled at a small table that was perhaps too near the bathroom and looked through a free paper while slowly eating my pastry. Buried in various adverts for workshops focusing on healing (general) and healing (specific), I was alerted by a falling chunk of candied apple that today marked a Friends of the Library book sale. I wrote the address in my notebook and, seeing the night's failed mapping, added the apple turnover in the Ojai circle. I looked up to see a man delivering a breakfast burrito to the table next to me and added a negative mark by the pastry. Leaving the café, I was nearly run over by a van from whose passenger window the woman who had been behind me flipped me off.

Walking off my breakfast, I searched the strip for the library book sale, which it turned out was housed in a portable building, something like I once had to finish the school year out in after the school I was going to was rented out and repurposed as a Spring business training retreat. The first year we were gleeful, believing that school was over until we saw, parked in columns and rows along the football field, aluminum portable classrooms. When I stepped inside the library, everything came rushing back—how the winters were excruciatingly cold, how nobody, the teachers included, wanted to stay in those cold buildings, and how sometimes we could see our breath in the mornings before our collective body heat warmed the aluminum room. It soon transpired that everyone tried to get out of going to class, from infirmity—licking palms, feigning fever, and purposeful self-poisoning—as in the case of one teacher, it was claimed, who at mid-term had gone insane after seeing ghosts for a week in his classroom. Although later it turned out that his hallucinations and temporary insanity was due more to an inadvertent chemical reaction between a formaldehyde solution sprayed onto the backs of the paneling and the cheaply and questionably produced insulation, and, as the two chemicals slowly interacted, it produced a gas that resulted in widespread low results on state-wide end-of-year exams. Unconsciously, I held my breath while compulsively browsing the library book sale, and finding nothing of interest on the shelves, I went over and asked the woman crewing the stamp pad and cigar box if she'd seen the man in the picture, if he had ever come in.

Well, I don't know, what's his name? she asked, with an eyebrow raised.

Mann, I said. Carl Mann. Or was. He might have changed it.

I don't understand, did you change it?

How could I?

I don't get it.

I'm working for this lawyer—a fraud case—and I just need to find him. Or not. I'm not quite sure.

Is this some sort of reality show?

I'm a detective, I said and tried to explain, sheepishly telling her about what I considered my primary job and then replied yes to the inevitable follow-up question, and said, a few, and I don't think you've heard of them.

Oh, I get it, she said and adjusted herself in the chair. A lot of writers come through here, and a lot of them just decided to settle down here, she said. This is just such a vibrant community. But it reminds me, have you ever heard of Caroline Mints? Oh, if you've never read anything by her, you have to she is absolutely the best writer around, or elsewhere, in my opinion. You know, I was going to reread *The Miracle of the Carmel Marriage Carousel*, but left it at home by the door because my dog, Artie, just couldn't bear to see me go, so I had to tire him out a little in the back yard playing fetch—he's so peculiar about what stick he wants to use—but by then I was late to open up here and so just left it there by the door. I could kick myself because I hate starting a new book before I've finished the last one. Well, let's see what we still got left here. I recommend her to everyone, so they go pretty fast. Hard to keep her on the shelf.

She got up from the folding canvas chair behind the folding plastic table and walked over to a small shelf of mass market paperbacks, all emblazoned in soft pastel colors with often shimmering gold and silver lettering. Among them I noticed a familiar title, but didn't feel any impulse to pick it up. You know the thing I like most about Caroline Mint's books? They tell a story. And not only just a story but she incorporates this little town and its history and everyone here. All the characters are just so real! You can open up one of her books and recognize all the people who live here, right off the bat. I swear two books ago, I was in it—it's called, *The Mysterious Looking Well of Pleasure*, and there was this library to a tee, and there I was right in this seat, and I'm the one who recommends the book to Doreen, and Doreen, who is almost certainly Rachel in real life, works at the hair salon, poor thing, but in the book she's working at the nail salon, and she reads a diary written by her great-grandmother that leads to her discovering 'the lost well of pleasure' right in the basement of the high school gym, where they were having a class reunion...but if you ask me, I think it's in the basement of the main branch of the library, but that's how she meets her long lost love, can you believe it, and becomes mayor—now I can't say it's *all* based in reality, I mean, one look at the mayor and that becomes clear as a bell, or 'clear as a bell on a winter day,' as I say in the book. And you know, poor Rachel, well that's all I can say, poor Rachel. Whenever someone comes in, I think, now is that Caroline Mints? I mean, she doesn't have a picture of herself on her books, and I just know she's been in here. I mean, how could she not have been, as good as she described me? If I ever found out, I wouldn't say anything at all; I'd just smile and know that it was Caroline Mints browsing my little shelves. I do know that she doesn't have a library card, not in town anyway, and if she did, I would read every single book she checked out. I even looked up the other name she used to write under, Caryl Hannah, which she wrote her *El Camino Romances* series—you know I never thought about how passion is not a car and it's not a truck before? I just wish she'd tell me that she knows that I know that she's here. I don't know why she wouldn't. I've been such a faithful reader that she owes me at least that, doesn't she? Some kind of acknowledgement. Is that too much to ask? I mean really. She turned with her hands on her hips and scanned the room for a few moments then suddenly plucked a yellow paperback from the shelf. Now this isn't one of ours, she said, it was from after her Caryl Hannah books, but before she moved here, and even though it's no *Looking Well*, or *Miracle*, and even though it's a guy's name, you can still tell it's her. She handed me the book. It was titled, *Avalanche*, but had a tropical scene on its cover. She walked back over to the folding table and looked at a sheet taped to the tabletop. Ok, so, that's a green dot, is that right? It's from the M shelf—I put it there to show her that I know it's really her—and so that'll be a quarter. I paid her and put the paperback in my pocket. Now, listen, she said, if you like that one, come back, and if you donate it back to us, you can get a dime credit and that way, you can get one of the good ones.

Okay, I said and thanked her.

Oh, do you have a card?

Do I need a library card?

No, a business card.

No, actually, I don't. I've only taken cases from my friend before now.

Well you should get some, she said, If someone like me wanted to hire you, how do I do that?

Hire me for what?

To find Caroline Mints, she said.

I thought about it for a minute. It would certainly be an easy job. I'm on a case right now, I said, as you know. But when I'm done with that, perhaps I'll stop by again.

All right, she said, it's a date! You should move here! You'd love living here, and I think she'll come in here one day, and I know I'll just recognize her and then I'll point her out for you.

Okeydokey, I said.

As I was walking towards Torito, I noticed a woman with a headset and metal detector slowly backing out of the brush. I stood there, transfixed by her total absorption in the process as well as her total sartorial commitment. She wore large rubber boots, cargo pants, a flannel shirt, and a vest full of pockets. I liked, too, that she wore a kind of utility belt, from which hung and jangled a flashlight, some sort of pointer tool, two knives, a spade, and a large leather pouch the size of a record sleeve. As she neared, I could hear the squeals from the headset. Then she swung around suddenly, the disk at my feet, Excuse me, she said. I stepped back, and she hovered the disk over where I had been standing. Listen to that squeak, just listen to that, she said. That's got to be gold, you hear how strong that is? She handed me the headset. The volume and high frequency levels were too abrasive for me. She set the instrument aside and pulled out the pointer tool, which turned out to also be a metal detector. It's right there, she said. And with the knife carved a neat circle around the edges of the signal and then flipped the dirt with the spade. Poking around again with the pointer, she found a small coin. She rubbed it on her leg and held it up to me. Take a look.

I held it in my hand. It was heavier, it seemed, than something like that should have been. The surface of it was hard to make out. I always imagined holding some kind of old coins, yet, when I looked at the thing in my hand, I felt a little sad. I handed it back.

I was hoping it was gold, but silver ain't bad, it ain't bad, she said. It'll clean up nice, it looks like...Seventeenth Century Dutch, it looks like to me. And that's a real one. See how thick it is? A few years back a guy claimed to find a bunch of treasure, and it was all silver and gold, for sure, stamped, but it was all too thin. That's a detail people don't get. Weight. It's all about the weight.

Did you say, Dutch? Someone drop it you think?

Nope, shipwreck.

Shipwreck? I looked around. The ocean was nearby, but still a ways off. We were in the mountains after all. How is that? I didn't know the water was this far. Did they build a dam? Do they build dams on oceans?

No. It's crazier than that. I mean, not many people believe it. But the thing I like about doing this is the history, you know. You find some strange little bit of history—a ship, a battle, a wagon train, or what have you. Go to the archives and look up everything you can, letters, old maps, what have you. That's where you look.

I've never thought of it. The detecting part of metal detecting.

Oh yeah, otherwise it's just going in the dark and then it's beer cans, beer cans, and more beer cans. She pulled a microfiber cloth out of the large pouch, dampened it with some kind special liquid, and was rubbing the coin with it. So I was in this library, and I came across an old story about a Dutch colony in Argentina. It was during the Anglo-Dutch War. It didn't last long, only six months or so. But in that time, they pulled out chest after chest of silver. Smelted and minted it right there and loaded it on a ship. Now, most books say it was lost at sea. But I found a letter that wasn't sent that claimed that they had seen a ship that had wrecked right here, on land.

How?

Well, how else? They put it on wheels. The Vikings did the same thing. Imagine, a Dutch ship loaded with silver from Argentina. It ran aground. Fearing the Spanish, they put it on wheels and sailed it inland, only to wreck again here, in Ojai. And when they move that tin can over there, I'll find a treasure trove out here, she said. She picked up the detector. Here, you can have this one; I mean, you were standing right on it.

No, I couldn't.

Go ahead, she said, There's lots out here, a whole ship's worth. Let this be your brush with history.

Thank you, I said. She put her headset back on and continued slowly waving the metal detector around as if our conversation had never happened.

Back in the car, I put the coin in the pocket in the back of my notebook. Added points to the map and reflected on it all. What steps to take next. I could go back to the observatory and ask around about Clinnemann, but I felt that wouldn't get me anywhere. I thought about expensing a metal detector and outfit like hers, then join the detectorist in her search. It was still detecting, wasn't it? Still billable? But then, thought better of it. I cringed at the idea of disturbing such a perfect obsession as she had. I thumbed through the paperback, not reading anything, and a card fell out—obviously used as a bookmark, which, I noticed, wasn't too far into the book. It said: Admit One—The Cranefly Fine Arts Museum. Why not, I said. I hadn't found the man here, only a few traces of him if I count everything, and was, more or less, at an end. Why not take a vacation? Torito spit gravel despite my best intentions, and we were off on the handsome highway driving further into the mountains towards the desert, the sun setting behind us, the evening growing before us.

V

AFTER A FEW HOURS OF DRIVING, the world turning from the marvels of Ojai to the marvels of the desert, I stopped at a gas station to feed Torito and look for a road atlas. It was a cement building with four pumps out front, one broken. Pay before you pump. All the posters and ads in the window were bleached cyan. The reluctant clerk looked at me for a while, suspicious of my interest in an atlas at this hour or ever, and had me follow him to an old storage closet to find one. It was priced less than a dollar, and I thought I'd found a marvel of antiquity, yet saw at the bottom that it had been printed from a trip mapping website and may not contain all the roads. I worried that the clerk would be forlorn, but Torito's rapacity for gasoline and my appetite for iced coffee and snacks for the coming days of driving made up the difference.

The Cranefly Museum of Fine Art, it turned out, was more of a once opulent mansion later converted to a museum. It was strangely situated alone on a plot of land that had, no doubt, once been far from the road and the city it connected, but after years of development, the dulcet country mansion now clashed with the prefab surroundings in a ludicrous way. There was little landscaping left that wasn't consumed by the parking lot.

I showed the ticket to the ticket taker standing by some red velvet ropes. Are you kidding, she said, This thing is ancient: it's like, from when I was born. Did you get this from your grandparents or something? I'm going to have to get my boss to see if it's even good anymore. She held the ticket in the air, took a picture of it with her phone, typed something, took a picture of me, typed something, then continued typing, smiling and laughing as she slid off the seat and disappeared through a door. Soon, another woman appeared. She wore her hair up, with a black suit jacket, a black sweater and black skirt with tall black boots and red tights. Hello, she said. My name is Janet. This is quite an artifact you have here. This was from before we issued these with expiration dates. We used to see a lot of them when we were transitioning, but about ten years ago I thought we'd seen the last one. It's almost a museum piece itself. She laughed. We might even put it on the wall. Often, people who bring them in also consider making a donation, she said, because they understand the value of an institution like this one.

Can I buy a guide instead?

She took a guide from a stack behind her, handed it to me, and rung me up, frowning a little when I handed her the black credit card.

Enjoy your visit, she said, walking away.

I read the guide as I walked:

Public entrance Lobby. To the left you find the Yellow Room.

OPPOSITE DOORWAY: *The Broken Tongues of Amel & Ameleta,* watercolor thought lost by J.P.M. Costener (English 1765-1815). Found aboard the *Três Pegas de Netuno*, a Portuguese Man of War, having been looted from the English sloop where Costener had been employed as ship's mate. The lightness of the medium is in contrast to the subject matter: the image of an angel with two heads and dressed in robes of what might be called a harlequin, except for the objects of judgment, punishment, or reward in the angel's hands. Said to be a depiction of the hermetic androgyne found in *Chemical Secrets of Nature* (1687) authored by M. Majer, a noted English Alchemist, while others point to the muddied edges of the robe and wings that seemed to have been painted later, covering the just perceptible images of the moon and sun, as well as a cave and three children riding an ox as proof that the image was originally an erotic sketch made for the amusement of the crew.

ON THE FARTHER WALL, TO THE LEFT: *A Watery Night in Amber and Grey,* by Herman Milton (American 1819-91), who was at a crossroads mid-career with early success as a landscape painter but was a moral failure, with a wife, a daughter, and another child on the way when he made the first sketch for the painting in 1846. Moving away from landscape, but not adept at portraiture, he discovered a method of composition exploiting geomancy and refraction. The exact details of his process are lost except for the small clue from the diary of eccentric social-ite, Kora Derringer, which explains that this method involved the setting up of a number of mirrors and colored globes (tinted paraffin films). The first example of this technique is *Watery Night,* a work Ruskin called, Pathetic and repugnant, a pot of rancid butter and slop thrown in the delicate face of beauty.

ON THE FAR RIGHT OF THIS WALL: an earlier painting by Milton, *Discord in Red and Brown: Misfortune on the Trail,* a simplistic landscape of its time.

BETWEEN THE MILTONS, CENTER OF THE EAST WALL: *Mme. Chapman,* a portrait by Edgar Frances Allen (American 1809-1849), painted in 1838. The sitter, although having commissioned the work, is said to have refused it, claiming Allen took pains to distort her figure in order to accommodate his own philosophy. Mme. Chapman was the widow of a late shipping baron who imported cotton and other wares through the East India Trading Company. Known mostly in Boston, Allen often made trips to New Orleans. It was on one of these trips that he met the elderly Mme. Chapman and presumably where the painting was first discussed. Earlier, in 1834, Allen was said to have joined a small enclave of intellectuals and mystics living outside of the Garden District who maintained that man could only be understood through a system of symbols found throughout history and nature. At the time of the first meeting, the group was working on compiling a lexicon for the understanding and usage of these symbols. It was a nearly impossible task, however, because each symbol varied according to its proximity to another symbol and symbol set of its receptor. While complicated, the task still had a predictable end, that is, until 1836 when it was discovered that some symbols were in fact non-symbolic and functioned more like grammatical markers, setting the project back nearly to its beginning. These grammatical markers played a role in deter-mining the relationship of the symbols it modified and thus the overall meaning of each symbol was conditional to its non-symbolic marker, so that as each symbol was discovered, it first had to be sorted out whether it was functioning as a symbol or non-symbol marker before the lexicon could be updated. Allen was immediately drawn in by the project contributing several diagrams and illustrations for the never published reference book. His contributions are largely lost except for some rough drafts found in a sketchbook, pages of which are on display in the Short Gallery. For the next decade, Allen's work turned to the macabre. Some speculated that it was owed to his association with the group; others, however, have dismissed this claim and see his later work to be an attempt to sell his work by exploiting the zeitgeist of the time to pay off his considerable debts. In October of 1849, Allen was said to have entered a waterfront tavern where a few years before he had given the portrait of Mme. Chapman to pay his tab and collapsed, apparently dead of rabies like so many members of the group.

ABOVE THE ENTRYWAY: *Love and Hate* by Wicek Fiołkoworóżowy. A Fauvist claustrophobic neo-noir scene of a brooding figure in the foreground of a room decorated with flowers and stars on the ceiling, a worn leather bag at the figure's feet; in the midground a large cat on a flower stand cleans itself, and in the background there is a feminine figure silhouetted in a lit doorway; all depicted in shades of purple, red, and blue.

HIGH ON THE WALL OF THE TELEPHONE ALCOVE: *Chancel de Marie,* by Prudence Arnica (English 1869-1954) a depiction of the artist's companion at the house of writer, Mitchell Meriwether (pseudonym Randall Constants, 1879-1970), who was at the center of a group of painters and writers who, during the early years of the XXc, were determined to assert the idea that art, whether written or painted, was to be experienced then discarded. The writers published largely on acidic newsprint purposely bound into frail boards with a wicking paste; the painters used a vehicle that bonded poorly, and while was at first fast and bright, dulled and chipped within the year leaving a thin cotton canvas. Because of this materiality, it is common for the group to be mistakenly considered to promote a communist or socialist ethos; however, its members were largely of upper-class European stock who often were outspoken supporters of high culture and elitism; many later sided with fascists during the Second World War, only to be interred and, in at least half the cases, to have been executed. Chancel, it is rumored, escaped a similar fate by being imprisoned in South America on a charge of looting, for most of the war, and consequently is one of the few contemporary works in the collection.

Across the Public Entrance Lobby, THE BLUE ROOM

The pictures here are of the XIXc, many of them by artists who were friends or acquaintances of Mr. Derringür.

THE SOUTH WALL, LEFT OF THE DOORWAY: *Madame Perchance Millett, the painter's mother,* by Marcel Millett (French 1832-83). Painted sometime in 1867 or 1871. Kept by Marcel until 1887 when it was thought lost but rediscovered in 1917 under a later painting of an old man followed by a retinue carrying a large, illuminated book that is perhaps three times their height. Deemed not painted by Millett but used by a student for an exercise.

Below: *Encre de Poulpe,* a sketch by the same artist depicting the patron of a Parisian café, painted several years later than the portrait above. The name of the person represented is not known, but speculations range from a one-time lover, Aidan Stein; Kinbote Green, a critic; or a late portrait of Julien Veber, a mystic. Unfortunately, Millett's style in this sketch is so poor that no identification can be definitive.

ON THE EAST WALL TOWARDS THE WINDOW: *Rien plus que le Déjeuner,* by Jean Reál Corcelle (French 1796-1875). Part of the short lived and largely prescient school of the Forma Organica Naturalis movement, whose contributions were minor, being made up of a small group of poets and painters, who, it was rumored, also made company of the pirates that used a nearby chain of small islands for a stopping-over point. Many of their works have been lost, painted over by forgers for their aged canvas or otherwise destroyed, with only a few examples surviving from Corcelle and the painter Serr Riggøn, who, in believing in self-manifestation of organic form, consequently sought to create works that would initiate rather than instruct. *(Strangely this painting appeared at first to be nothing but a blank canvas, tinted slightly blue or green given the age, but when one slowly moves around the painting, one gets the impression, though not quite, of figures in a drawing room—one of them in typical early 19th century clothing, the other, appearing more effeminate, was dressed in the Romantic style: slightly open flowing blouse, roguish leggings, and wild hair, but as one tries to get a more accurate impression, it once again vanishes into the plane of color.)*

WINDOWED (NORTH) SIDE OF THE ROOM, EAST FACE OF THE PROJECTING WALL, NEAR THE CRAWLSPACE: *Basque Peasant Amusing a Tiny Dog,* by Bartleby Henry Shaw (American 1856-1925) portrait sketch in oil. *(The peasant looked remarkably peasant-like and the dog remarkably like a* *dog, I thought, though they both seemed to be patiently refusing some order issued off-canvas.)*

ACROSS ON THE NORTH FACE OF THE PROJECTING WALL: *In the Beauty of the Lost Goss of Glossvelier,* by Amijl Amerith (pseudonym) (unknown approx. 1850-1920). This striking work by the anonymous painter known only by a pseudonym, depicts an exchange of some sort between two figures. Incorporating elements of masonic ritual, and intimations of the Bear-girls of Brauron, some scholars believe it to be a color sketch for a production of *Die Zauberflöte*, the set of which was destroyed in a barge fire near Ibiza.

ACROSS ON THE WEST FACE OF THE PROJECTING WALL FACING NORTH: *Omnibus Button Drop,* by Erena Monkino (French 1903-1976). Previously attributed as a much earlier painting, *Rays of the Star,* by Hunstman the Younger, and later considered a poor forgery of its misattribution. It was only recently that its true attribution was discovered.

All of the works were intriguing, but it was this last painting that caught my eye. And there in the painting I saw, improbably, a man's face, appearing to be made up in silver make-up, barely seen in a shadow. I held up the picture I was given and there was more than a passing resemblance. There were two possibilities—one, and more a fancy—was that Mann had traveled back in time; after all, there had been a strange proliferation lately of paintings and photographs that seemed to portray figures out of time—a man in a tee shirt and sunglasses witnessing the funerary caissons of Lincoln passing; a tramp-like figure in a Chaplin film apparently talking on a touch-screen smart phone; and a series of celebrities seemingly appearing in tintypes and cyanotypes. Fearing the former, I took to the latter possibility of a contemporary addition, and I walked to the side of the painting, trying to catch the brushstrokes along the canvas, and it seemed to me, although I'd learned I tend to succumb to a level of fantasy, that the brush strokes where the figure was looked newer and somewhat tighter, whereas the rest of the painting had a slow and steady building up of surface. But in either case, it seemed to me, there was nothing but this strange trace of Mann and to no end. Was he, like in the painting, in the shadows of a market somewhere? I looked up the painting in the guide and saw that it was painted originally in Boston, and so, finding no alternative, decided it was as good a place as anywhere else to go. I could, according to the atlas, take the Freedom Walk. I was nervous, however, about the state of the muscle car after such a long drive but endeavored nevertheless to have my vacation.

On my way out, I purchased a reproduction of the painting in postcard form. It wasn't until I was at a traumatically filthy rest area that I noticed that in the place of the figure, there was instead a young woman holding an orange in one hand and pointing to the heavens with the other, and although the card was small and the resolution strangely pixelated, it occurred to me that it was not a reproduction of the painting I had just seen, but, as noted on the verso, was a painting by the same artist, owned by, of all strange institutions, the Maxwell Browne Museum of Natural History. After exhausting my wet naps, I quoted one of my professors: mistakes are just misunderstood opportunities, and after a shower in a slightly less filthy motel room, I plotted my drive there.

VI

WHEN I FIRST ARRIVED AT THE NOW NAMED, MaBoNaHMu, located in a township outside of Boston, I thought I'd made a mistake—it was like a theme park: there was the Archimedes Adventure Water Slide, an obstacle course called the Darwin Danger Derby, the twisting Newton's Commotion Coaster, and the Galileo Suicide Sling Shot. I went to the booth and paid a fifty-dollar contribution for a one-day pass, which was good on the classic rides and all of the exhibits, but none of the special exhibit rides. I had to go through a metal detector and the guard looked suspiciously at my pen and notebook, curious why I had those when everyone else had phones. Is it poison, he asked.

No, I said, it's just a pen.

Is it a knife? he asked, or one of those spy guns?

Just a pen, I said and I took out my notebook and drew a small boat.

All you can do is write with it? You can't even use it as a stylus on a tablet?

Just a pen, I said.

It's not even a USB drive or something?

Nope, I said.

Whatever, as long it's not a knife or a gun, he said, and waved me through the turnstile.

The inside of the Maxwell Browne was considerably more crowded than the Cranefly. It was full of neon, dance music, a number of gift shops with groups of tourists, and in the tumult of groups of parents with their young children running and weaving between the empty double-wide strollers, many of the parents were pushing groups of disaffected school children, all moving along a series of lines on the floor, each depicting a possible path through the museum, each with his or her own mascot. There was Radical Raccoon who had a glam rock look, Awesome Aardvark who had a skateboard, Hip-Hop Hippo who carried a boom-box and was decked out in breakdance gear, Millennial Mongoose who had an assortment of 'smart' gadgets, and Snooty Snail who wore broken glasses and carried books somehow.

I looked for some kind of indicator of which path I should take and went to the gift shop where they directed me to a guide for twenty-five more dollars. I tried to look up paintings in the index, but there were only coupons in the back. I then asked one of the 'Experience Engineers'—signified by the red knit shirt, tan shorts, and pith-helmet—and showed him the postcard, Well, I've never seen it, but if it's here, it'll probably be the Snooty Snail path; it takes you through the old exhibits. But I've never gone down it, so I don't really know.

I thanked him and set off on the Snooty Snail path, but was almost immediately swept into a tour group led by a shorter man, dressed in the Experience Engineers outfit—but with a placard around his neck that was inscribed *volunteer*, whose voice I had to strain to hear, which was almost impossible because of the children, who the guide pointed out were the backing band and entourage of the pop star, Sylvia Platte, who unsurprisingly, I'd never heard of. We moved along slowly through what was feeling less like a museum and more like a product convention at a nightclub, stopping at each brightly lit and equally crowded exhibit displaying for the most part how brand-named products are made, or work, in the contrasted low light of the museum. At each one the small man muttered a few things about each product, gesticulating or attempting a kind of pantomime by variously inflating his cheeks and sucking in his cheeks into a pucker. I couldn't hear what he said, but I was able to gather from various phones around me and pieced together from their various text windows that it was something about someone (it was unclear who) being a cutting edge and epic contribution. Then someone laughed, He said digital. Another kid said, He said epic, and laughed. And I laughed, and then they looked at me. I decided to push through the crowd to get closer to this Experience Engineer, thinking perhaps that he might know where the painting was.

It took some time, trying to synchronize my advance with the slower advance of the crowd through the tunnels of tanks. Finally, I got close enough to hear him as we neared a smaller exhibit, the first to either not be sponsored by or about a product of a major company. It was a tank full of water displaying a rather awkward looking fish (for this the Experience Engineer offered no impersonation) that looked to be an assemblage of a number of boring fish but composed in such a jumbled way—a baffling fin that jutted improbably backwards and askance, the eyes recessed under Shar-Pei like skin rolls that would weirdly balloon when it swam forward, which was only occasionally; it seemed, preferring to swim backwards and upside down. It was only when the strange fish unexpectedly flattened itself and, using the baffling fin, spun, like a run-away Frisbee, to the sandy floor of the tank near a fake treasure chest and a number of old looking urns, that the crowd of children nearest to the Experience Engineer surged backwards enough that I was able to take advantage of an opening and move close enough to catch what the he was saying: ...was discovered by the famous naturalist, Dr. Christopher Moore. As a young man, Moore dreamed, as many of you perhaps do, of having a species named after him, one of the greatest honors in a scientist's life. All around him, in books and later working at the university, people were discovering new species; it was a very exciting time to be working. Moore, eater, ugh, eager for the same distinction, would teach for one semester then head a number of research expeditions all over the world, to the farthest recesses of the jungle, to the least trod dunes of deserts, spending his days exploring the depths of caves, and though of a weak constitution for it, spent time in the depths of the oceans and seas. He studied avidly the whole range of natural sciences and became expert in many families of life on this planet. Because of this encyclopedic expertise, Dr. Moore's lectures are legendary and now, thanks to the generous people at Wild Things Audio, are available for purchase on cassette in the Maxwell Brown Museum of Natural History gift shop, just to the left of the Concessions Corral. Still, Dr. Moore was always beaten to the mark when it came to discovering some living thing that hadn't already been described. The years passed in his Ivy Tower, and his dreams seemed to have faded. He took fewer trips, he lectured more, and eventually took on far more classes than a man of his age would in normal circumstances. He continued to publish, and although the articles were erudite and maintained an encyclopedic seasoning, the flair, the panache for which he was known, was noticeably bland. The advent of a more genetics-based science eventually made his classes something of a novelty for the incoming students. His books were legendary, his lectures stuff of lore, but now, like a legend, he was being outgrown. He paused and looked around at the crowd of children whose downcast faces were now all brightly lit by their phones.

Dr. Moore, the man continued, spent much of his time with the undergraduates, often dining in the school cafeteria where he was treated like a celebrity, with no lack of awed freshmen cramming their pea green institutional trays wherever there was space on the institutional mauve tabletop, except one day, a very important day in Dr. Moore's life it turned out. You see, that day, students had decided to stage a sit-in protest, demanding that not just a vegetarian menu, but a selection of vegan meals be offered on campus, where 'students were given credits to eat, but no credit as eaters.' The action effectively closed the cafeteria that day. Dr. Moore decided to spend his lunch walking. He walked around the campus for a little while, then ventured towards the town square, which consisted of a large park bordered by small shops. Dr. Moore sat on a bench in the park and stared out at all the people sitting on blankets and benches, and the children sitting on the edge of the fountain letting the water splash on them. He could name every species of bird, every tree; he could recite to himself the life cycle of every gnat that quietly pestered the laughing couples sharing their lunch. He started to get hungry and walked into the first sandwich shop he encountered, one of the many that seemed to pop up overnight like mushrooms, then disappear just as soon, each one serving some variation of a simple meal between slices of bread.

The sandwich shop was small and had, as the professor wrote, a sharp spicy smell to it that rested like oil on top of a more abrasive scent of clumsily-used cleaning fluids. The professor was a little tentative in his selection because his stomach had been a little delicate in recent months, and the dishes had names that seemed counter to describing the meals. In the end, he chose one called, 'the flower-headed carnival mitt' which, for some reason, he thought was most likely to be vegetarian. He took the nicely-wrapped sandwich and a bottle of sassafras soda (a minor passion), and walked back to the bench where he began eating.

The sandwich just tasted like salty mayonnaise, making it a thankless task to eat. Undaunted, the old man took larger bites to hurry the experience, washing each nearly un-chewed bite down with great swallows of his sassafras soda, until he started choking. He waved his hands at the pigeons, he waved his hands at the ants, and he waved his hands at the lovers trading bites of possibly more scrumptious lunches until he fell off the bench and kicked his feet. He was choking. The guide pantomimed choking to death and one of the children shouted, Look, he's dying! And then all the rest of the children suddenly raised their heads and phones and took pictures and video, only to seem disappointed when the Experience Engineer had not collapsed in spasms but composed himself and continued, He didn't die, that wouldn't be a nice ending to this story, would it? No, fortunately, a bystander managed to call an ambulance in time. What had happened was a small bone had become lodged in his throat and it worked as a kind of crossbeam support for the mortar of hastily chewed food and he had to undergo immediate surgery. He was weakened by the procedure and had to stay in the hospital for a few days. Where did the bone come from? Well, the answer brings us closer to the end of this story. The sandwich that he ordered was not vegetarian, as he had hoped, but a kind of fish fillet with greens. A very bland fish, at that, so bland that it hid in the flavors of the other toppings. In the meantime, consummate naturalist that he was, he asked the doctor who performed the surgery for the offending bone. Usually, such a request was not granted, but since this was the University Hospital and the patient the famous Dr. Moore, the nurse came in shortly and gently laid a delicately small bone in the old professor's hand. He examined it carefully in the light, running through countless exemplars of fish anatomies stored away in his mind, and found there was an abnormal texture and curve to the bone he held. He immediately called his TA, a young graduate student, and asked for every fish guide he could get his hands on, in his office or in his library, to be brought to the hospital room along with as many of the sandwiches as the young man could buy.

When the young TA arrived, he found the professor more bright-eyed than he had ever seen him in class or in conference. Although he had an I.V. taped to his forearm, was dressed in a gown, and had a tube down his bandaged throat, Dr. Moore seemed like a young man. When the TA handed him the sandwiches, vaguely perplexed, he was further confused by the Professor pulling apart each sandwich in turn, probing the lame fish fillet with his fingers, the I.V. snaking along with each movement, until he held to the light two small bones resting in his palm. The TA saw nothing more than slimy fish bones, but acquiesced to the old man's expertise, saying, in a somewhat patronizing tone, yes, Professor, it is a marvelous find. For the remainder of his hospital stay Dr. Moore pored over books, holding the small bones in his hand, making jagged notes, and with the close of each book, his excitement rose; with each volume exhausted, his cheeks became rosier, his heart pumped harder, and his suspicion of the nurses and doctors grew. Each time someone entered the room, he hid the bones within the starched white sheet, or slipped them in the pages of a book, and even once, hid them in his mouth, smiling and nodding or shaking his head to each question.

When Professor Moore was well enough to leave the hospital, he went directly to the little sandwich shop near the park and the scene of his near death only to find that the shop had been closed down by the health department and the Fish, Game, and Wildlife Commission. Dr. Moore was once again crushed. His efforts to keep the discovery secret had backfired. He could have sent his sample to the shop, to interview the owners about where they got their fish, what fish they served, and slowly, meticulously, scientifically, traced the bizarre bone back to the body of the fish; instead, there he was, an old professor standing before an empty store front. He cupped his hands and peered in, but there were only overturned chairs, a few tables with the putrefying remains of old sandwiches, and catsup graffiti.

He returned to his office on campus, which had become more of a home than his small bungalow just a mile away, having moved most of his books, his reading chair and lamp, his desk, the most often worn selections of his wardrobe, his house shoes, a small refrigerator, an antique liquor cabinet, coffee maker, and a large trunk filled with the various outfits and souvenirs of his world travels into his office. He flipped on the lamp, changed into his house slippers, settled into his reading chair, took out the little bones, and stared at them; how insignificantly small they looked in his palm, yet how easily their spiny awkwardness could have been the foundation for his oblivion or immortality. He thought about swallowing them again. Such were the baroque thoughts of the old man, such was the angle of his descent, feeling a little bit smaller in his chair, his feet fitting a little looser in his slippers, the books, a little heavier in his lap. Suddenly there was a knock, and the TA burst into the gloomy office and presented a sheet of paper to the old man. Dr. Moore, who just minutes before was ready to let the little bones finish the job, couldn't believe his teary eyes. In his hands he held the official declaration of his discovery. He looked up at the TA with wet, questioning eyes.

During his first visit with the old professor in the hospital, the TA, not entirely ready to discount the old man as finally having gone off his rocker, decided to take some of the meat from each sandwich to the Genetics Department at the university and to a young geneticist graduate student he had a crush on and asked her to extract and compare any salvageable DNA from each sample. She agreed, but on the sole condition that the young TA would repay her with one home-cooked meal and wine.

As the young geneticist went to work with what fortunately turned out to be uncooked fish, the TA cleaned his apartment, deciding then to throw out a good amount of his possessions that had been accumulating slowly over the years, like the diorama of taxidermal frogs in the pose and dress of a yacht-rock band and the litter of carefully bundled stacks of ATM receipts, the ink on many of them already vanished.

That weekend they dined. The TA cooked chicken with basil, lemon, and capers as a main dish and red potatoes lightly seasoned with butter and rosemary, and lightly wilted kale as sides. He served a cheap white wine that was a little fruity, but worked well enough with the meal. But it wasn't until the couple was halfway through the more expensive dry chardonnay the geneticist brought up the topic of the DNA tests. Most of the samples had been the same, a type of koi, but that three of them had been slightly different—in the same family, yes, closely related, yes, but not the same fish at all. In fact, she said, it was kind of weird because the three samples seemed to belong to a kind of 'genetic throwback' of the other samples. In fact, she said, it was as if, somewhere along the way, the odd switch had been turned back on here and there along the genetic code, but while the more evolved switches were still on. She said, finally, The fish in situ must look absolutely monstrous.

After a little more research, a few emails and a few more phone calls, the TA was able to procure, with the requisite furtiveness, several samples from a left-over supply of questionably harvested fish, and with the DNA evidence, submitted them as a new species while the professor convalesced.

And now we will always remember Dr. Moore as the man who discovered the strange fish dubbed, 'The Lesser Moore' or, as it is more commonly called, 'The Spinning Platter Fish' which, the Experience Engineer added, is an exclusive holding of this museum.

By the time the Experience Engineer was done with the story, I was the only one still standing in the bright neon of the museum. Even 'The Lesser Moore' had disappeared under the sand or perhaps into the false treasure chest in the corner of the tank. I smiled at the Experience Engineer who shrugged and pointed to the corridor behind me, which, following the line on the floor, led to an even more brightly lit place beyond, then he turned and vanished behind a door marked, Employees Only. Soon I found myself in a safari-themed food court selling fried fish and calamari on sticks, corndogs (with sage relish), an assortment of multi-colored candied apples, oversized lollipops, and huge bushels of blue or pink cotton candy in leopard-print cones. A little hungry after such a long tour, I purchased fried calamari on a stick. When I reached in my jacket to pay, I noticed a note had been put there, possibly when I was so jostled by the crowd. The note read: *You're in Danger. We must talk. Door past the tank. M.* I sat down at one of the tables and took a bite only to discover that it wasn't seafood at all, but rather molded and deep-fried taffy. Looking around, taffy in greasy cherry or maybe strawberry flavored strands slowly drib-bling onto the paper plate, I noticed a woman standing near the cotton candy machine staring at me. She gave a few quick tilts of her head, then turned and went through the door marked Employees Only, and, once freed of the taffy, I followed. Through the door, I discovered that the tank wasn't filled with water, but only that the double-paned glass contained water, giving the illusion of being full, like a doll's bottle of vanishing milk; and below the sandy bottom, was a space for a controller of sorts, and there, draped on a hook, was the empty sequined felt body of The Spinning Platter Fish.

After having failed to properly follow the woman, and after having gone through a series of random turns and various labeled doors, and several distractions including a model of the proposed museum renovation that looked strikingly familiar—perhaps something from a painting I couldn't place, I found myself in the parking lot, with not a soul around. Likewise absent in the cobbled ocean of cars, was dear Torito. I figured the best way to find him was to walk around slowly in a spiral from the center of the lot, and to my dismay, it seemed that Torito had been stolen or towed. A nearby sign said the city was in charge of towing and to take up any complaints with Department of Motor Vehicles. I walked around the parking lot a little more, hoping I was wrong. At the end of the spiral was a bus stop, and the bus happened to stop at that moment, so I boarded, hoping that it would take me downtown, and hopefully, to the DMV, which was a strange place to see about a towed car. Meanwhile, I mapped the day in my notebook by drawing a circle and labeling it fish then, on a previous page, drawing a spiral starting at the place where the apexes of the two triangles, then moving counter clock-wise from there until reaching the outer edge of the inverted triangle, then making a point at each place where the lines intersected; I had no idea yet what each point was, however. Without thinking I pulled the signal cable for the next stop, then, feeling guilty about doing so, got off the bus.

VII

THE DMV AND ADJACENT CITY IMPOUND LOT was located in a strip mall with a nail salon on one side and a vaping café on the other. I sat in one of the plastic seats next to a man dressed in blue coveralls and sporting a handle-bar mustache. In his breast pocket, he had a pencil stuffed in among a number of loose notecards. I looked around at the signs in the office, which were in three languages: English, Spanish, and Marshallese. There were warnings in the three languages, prohibitions in three languages, but mostly there were advertisements in the three languages. When the light above the bulletproof glass lit up, I started to walk over to the administrator at the window, but the woman held up her hand, then pointed to a roll of numbers off to the side. I went over and pulled the tab to find number 474. The woman behind the glass yanked an antique microphone mounted off to the side and said, number three-six-two! Number three hundred and sixty-two. When I looked around, there were no other available seats, so I sat back down next to the man in coveralls, facing away a little, so as not to engage him, but not so much as to disturb the neighbor on the other side of me, who, like myself, was dressed in tan slacks and red windbreaker, but her ball cap said, *Anchors Away.*

Soon, I was very uncomfortable and had to shift my body, trying to be inconspicuous, but the man in coveralls smacked my arm with the back of his hand. I tried not to turn around, but he swatted me again, then said, My back hurts, your back hurt? You know why? The seat you're in is engineered to be uncomfortable, so you don't fall asleep. Not only that, but institutions spent a lot of money on this, brought in a lot of industrial psychologists, they're called. The man held his hands out in front of him trying to square something invisible, They bring in the government head-shrinkers and give them T-squares and they let them loose to draw up these things—all these different and subtle ways to make our life unbearable, to remove any pleasures in working, in learning, in life. They don't want us to get comfortable learning because then we might start to figure things out. They don't want us to get comfortable working because comfortable, in their minds, is the same as laziness. They figure that the more pissed off we get, the more we work to get the hell out of there, and we focus our energy in the only place it can go since the bosses are behind the door, protected by the security guards, and that is into greater productivity—everyone, bring on the productivity. A guilt trip that goes all the way back to Croatoan. Listen, you hate the chair, and you hate the boss, so you work faster to show them both! We'll do anything just to not sit in the damn things again. He laughed and pulled a handkerchief from his back pocket and blew his nose. All this air freshener damages the olfactory nerves. And recent research shows they lower the IQ, if you even believe in IQ. Excuse me. He blew his nose again. But see, he continued, then they make too many of these chairs, so they put them here in public offices too, so we don't fall ass asleep waiting in line. But see there are still too many of the chairs, so they sell them off cheap at cheap box stores, and of course we buy them because they're cheap and next thing you know, they are in your homes, right there at your dinner table and now they're everywhere—you snuggle them up to your TV tray, put them in your bedroom, you give 'em to the kids, and so now you go to work and sit in the uncomfortable things getting pissed off; go to fill out some cheap paperwork at some city building and sit in them getting pissed off; and then you go home pissed off, thinking that now you'll finally get some rest, but guess what, you're sitting in one of the chairs there too, even if you try to do everything on-line like they tell you, you got to still sit in one of these damn chairs. You go home sit there and steam because you can't figure why you're so upset and think the world's about to fall apart, and then, and then... you go to work the next day, miserable, and come home and again and again. Of course we begin to hate each other. We're upset all day and figure it can't be work, it can't be the chair, because everyone has these chairs. Because you are doing what everyone else is doing. It's a kind of Virtual Reality we end up living in. Everything here was once in someone's mind. I mean, literally; someone thought this world up, and because we're born into it, we think it's the way it should be, just like these chairs, that we deserve these uncomfortable chairs because if they were making us angry, they would have gotten rid of them long ago; if they were bad for us, they wouldn't sell them, right? He gave the one he was sitting in a little whack. A security guard walked over and said Sir, please respect the furniture, don't start hitting the furniture or I'll have to remove you. Then the guard returned to his post by the glass door.

This is why I said to myself, I said, Ros, you have to take off. You have to take—you and Ros, take your cats, get a bio-diesel RV and take off. The man laughed and leaned back in his chair, the plastic back bending, Smooth sailing on the highways, he said then darted out his arm, like he was trying to chop a fly, then said, but then they take that away. No, Ros, you and Ros and your cats, you're too free; you have it too figured out; you don't have any of those chairs in your RV; you threw them out, so here, we're gonna just take that away from you; you've been a little too hard to track. He laughed again. Now I'm here. Ros is at the shelter where they took our little kitties. Can you believe that? Ros can take care of Ros, but all those innocent little kitties? He was quiet for a while.

I took the opportunity to look around for another chair, but people were standing along the wall now.

Yup, he said, Look there, and pointed to an old woman in the corner, looking at the large opaque storefront windows, where you can hear the traffic, the people and trees moving behind the pea-green paint. That's our future, that's what the machine makes of you. Everyone knows that's what's coming, everyone, but everyone working here is too worried to say anything, feels too alone, too afraid of its truth. It's been called out over and over. You know what this is? It's the system that eats itself, he said, an ouroboros of time and misery. Tell me, guy: what's your future? Where do you stand in time?

Number three-six-four, the woman said from behind the glass, Three hundred and sixty-four; now come on people, you're only making everyone else wait longer! Ros got up from his chair saying,

Remember what I said. Here, he handed me a card, winked at me, twisted at his handle-bar mustache, then walked over to the teller window. The card was printed with the letters R.O.S., beneath it was a phone number. Nothing else. His seat was immediately filled by a man who looked a little like a sweaty Rutherford B. Hayes.

I looked around again, and it did seem like the whole office was irritable. No matter what forms you have completed, no matter how calm or obsequious you were, you were given different instructions and turned away to pluck another number from the roll and wait. The room was full of these turned-away people, and, looking closer at all the chairs they were sitting in, I saw that he was right, that everyone was turning and slouching, stuffing sweatshirts and jackets in the seats; and I, too, was now a member of the turned-away crowd who was sweating and stinking in the waiting room.

Well, fuck me, muttered a woman standing at the payphone, hanging up the receiver. She walked past me and turned to say, What is this world coming to? Let me ask you one question, only one thing in this world I want to know: why they got to make nothing sacred? Why do they have to take everything good in life? Every shining thing in life? Every little fucking thing, she said, turning and looking directly at me, and turn it around on you? Take, take, take, just keep taking whatever. She turned away from me and walked over to stand against the wall and joined the others straining to look through the opaque green window.

Number three-four-seven. Last call, three hundred and forty-seven. I checked and was still holding number 474. The man in the coveralls was no longer at the window, and I imagined him being reunited with his cats, driving down the highway, talking to himself in the third person. The smell of the nail salon was suddenly strong, and I was feeling a little lightheaded, so decided to find the restroom. My seat was snatched up by a woman who had a dog in her purse. The dog looked at me. I looked at the dog.

Urinals have held a particular interest for me. I particularly love urinals in old train stations; they're large, ornate, and sunk into the floor. Modern urinals, on the other hand, are small, too high, and shallow; they seem to be designed to spit piss back, not submit to it, and around any urinal there is graffiti. Above this mealy-mouthed urinal of the DMV was a phone number written in ballooning girl-ish script. To pass the time I repeated the number to myself in the fashion of different actors: Jimmy Cagney, Katharine Hepburn, Clint Eastwood, and Mr. Ed.

When I came back from the bathroom, number 347 was still at the one open window. Seeing the payphone nearby, I decided to dial the number in the voice of Errol Flynn. After a number rings a woman answered.

Hello, I said tentatively, this may seem strange, but I saw your number on the wall, and...

I see, the woman said.

I'm sorry. I'm sure you didn't want to know that your number was written on a wall somewhere.

Oh, no. I wrote it there.

Yeah? That's strange, I said. I mean, usually, that's...huh.

And you called it, she said slowly, don't you think that's strange?

Is this strange?

No, just a shock; you're the first person to call.

Really?

Yeah, you'd be amazed. I wrote it there like three months ago, she said. I guess it was kind of stupid to do—I mean, why not pay for a personals ad, right, or go online?

Right, that makes sense, I said. But did you write your name a lot of places or just at the DMV office?

Well, yeah; I figured all you have time on your hands, and, well there you go. Also, you'd definitely have a car, she said laughing.

I laughed too and said, Well, maybe if you had written something, like, I enjoy long walks on the beach, sunsets, dogs or cats, things of that nature. More people would have called.

Well, you called, she said.

Yes. Well, you've got me there.

Yes, I do, she said, and I don't want to squander the moment, so I want to get right to the point; let's get right into it, okay?

Into it?

Yeah, let's start with, I don't know, what is your name, and are you male or female?

A man?

A. Mann, she said, Anthony? Arnold, Armando? I'll say Armando, that's a nice name.

I meant, I'm Guy.

That your middle name? I don't need a middle name really, she said.

What is this...I, I don't get it...

I told you we're getting down to it, she said. You called me, remember, and I answered your call; I mean, the least you can do is answer a few questions for me, right, Armando? Now, I was born in Orange County, just a Valley Girl—so where were you born?

Isn't that the OC?

You're from the OC? Where's that?

No, Texas, I said, in this little town—once there were these pigs that...I thought the...

Pigs? Oh, that's crazy, ok. How tall are you?

...they kind of wrecked the town. Wait, what? I'm about six, maybe, five eleven...let's say six feet.

Average, she said, Just an average guy who can't read notes or follow instructions, am I right, Guy? Tell me, do you drink soda or coffee or tea?

All four.

Soda then. In the upcoming election, who will you vote for?

Vote?

You're from Texas, right? I'll put Republican.

But I live in San Francisco.

What are you doing in LA?

My car was towed.

Oh, bummer, she said, by who? Maybe you should have stayed in San Francisco. What kind of car?

Rental.

Is it American? Japanese? Korean? Dutch? Is it nice?

It is a kind of muscle car, I guess.

I put down that you lease a mid-range American car. Are you a balding middle-aged guy, Armando? Cruising around parking lots? I bet you are. Red windbreaker? I'll put that. How many hours do you spend a day watching television? What programs do you watch most?

I don't have a TV.

That's weird. Okay, but you must watch TV, like online or at the bar...most people, even if they say they don't watch TV, actually watch like up to ten hours a week. I'll put that down, ok? And you're an average guy, so I'll put sports. Football, right? No, you live in San Francisco, so I'll put, yuck, soccer. Armando? Can you name the last ten products you have bought, by their name brands?

What is this?

Don't worry, I'll fill that part in; I'll put some guy stuff down.

Down where? I said.

Ok, last one, she said.

Last what? I said.

Oh don't worry. It's not important. I'll just put Sylvia Platte; everyone loves them. Anyway, thank you for your time and have a great day and visit our website to leave feedback about your survey experience. And she hung up. The phone rang again as soon as I hung up.

Hello, a recorded voice said when I answered, thank you for taking our survey. You and your opinions are important to us. Please take a short survey about your survey experience to help us improve your future experience. You will be entered for a chance to win a new ebook.

I hung up the phone. It didn't ring again.

I went over to lean against the wall and, in the green light of the window, looked at the postcard of the painting again. I looked at the snapshot, and I felt there was a strange semblance. A sudden suspicion befell me, and I tried to imagine a handlebar moustache on the face in the picture, but it bore no resemblance to the man who had talked to me. I reviewed the notes I'd written and made a new map, gathering the words from the other maps that seemed then to be important. I looked at the triangles beneath the spiral. Once my number was called, I tried to explain myself to the unreceptive clerk before reluctantly paying the fine using the expense card and was soon reunited with Torito in the lot next door. But where were we going? The museum had been a bust. I flipped through the atlas and put my finger down at random and moved it in a clockwise spiral and then coaxed Torito out of the impound lot. It seemed, when I got on the road, that the little red muscle car had developed stomach problems since we last were together.

VIII

AFTER DRIVING ABOUT A HUNDRED MILES, Torito's cough got worse, until, limping and sputtering, we were able to pull into a service station off the highway, though just barely. The mechanic and I had to push the infirm beast into the garage. The car felt like it was covered in cold sweat. Welp, the mechanic said, I can't say what it is what's wrong with it. Looks like you got gas in the tank, so maybe it's the fuel injection, some rust on the spark plugs, distributor, or something of that sort, or could be any number of things. He spat tobacco into a cup, then took his hat off and wiped his brow with the back of the hand holding the cup. You know, I can't tell you anything until I get in there, look around, and see what kind of mess is going on. I mean, I can try to give you an estimate in, oh I don't know, thirty minutes or maybe an hour if you want to come back.

Well, I said, I'm not from around here. I mean, I don't have a hotel room or anything. I just barely pulled off the highway.

You can hang around. I would say take a walk somewhere but you're at a funny kind of time around here. All the eateries close at about three, and all the bars don't open until about six. He smiled and a tuck of brown crept out the side of his mouth. I guess they figure everyone wants to have dinner with their family or something. Towering example, ain't it?

In that case, could I get a few things from the car?

Sure thing.

I rummaged around Torito and got my notebook, the fountain pen, and the paperback that I'd bought in Ojai. Then it occurred to me, since I had it in my hand, to ask the mechanic if he'd seen the man I was looking for and showed him the photograph.

I don't get it, he said. Course I've seen him; is this a trick?

I couldn't believe my luck! When did you see him? I said.

When do you think?

I don't know, I said. Is he here now?

Look buddy, he exhaled, I just work on cars, maybe have a few beers at night, and I like it that way. Why don't you leave me out of whatever weird thing is going on here, ok? Show me a picture and ask me a dumb question about it; ok, do whatever you got to do, just I'm not interested in getting messed with, ok? If you leave me alone, I can get you back on the road in an hour maybe two. We got a little couch over there and some coffee and Danishes. You like Danishes?

You can't say any more about the man in the picture?

What else do you want me to say, buddy? I don't know where the cameras are, but you don't got my permission to film me, ok? Now if something is wrong with this car, I'll figure it out, and if I find you're wasting my time, I'm going to take it out in trade, you know what I mean?

I nodded and said, Yes, sorry. I didn't mean to trouble you. I'll wait in the office.

Uh-huh, the man turned and walked over to a younger man, and they started talking. The younger man laughed and shook his head.

I went into the office and found the coffee. I poured myself a cup and thought about how I offended the mechanic. I looked at the photograph, but it was the same one as always. I blew my breath into my palm: it could drop someone at a hundred yards. I tried to wipe my tongue with a napkin. I thought about apologizing to the mechanic for my bad breath, but opened the paperback of *Avalanche* I'd gotten in the library sale instead. I was feeling a little lost and started to read:

SWERVE THREE

I

THE FAUCET FLOWS; THE SHOWER RUNS. If only the super of this dump would fix the drain.

Here is my longstanding ritual: begin with a shave, followed by pushups on the bathroom honeycomb tile—today, a long-shot from my personal best—then undress for a cold rinse.

Prescribed by Jillian Carbess, the ritual is to manage my "thereins"— the nipping at my ankles from black dog bummers—drowning despondency—my tidal waves of personal *blah.*

She will be waiting beyond the shower curtain when I am finished— Headlight, my Maine Coon—an adept rodent darter on four white mittens, whose marbled tail flourishes between the legs of my trousers as we descend the stairs.

The off-kitchen balcony Headlight and I share overlooks Beachwood Canyon, not far from the Hollywood sign. Our treehouse is canopied by the boughs of untrimmed oaks and prosperous fruit trees, and the innumerable red berries of California Holly. The balcony, on which I fix gin and tonics, held the summer suicides of two previous tenants, and thusly Headlight consents to talk, long and often, as I mange my "thereins" with the well-stropped razor, vigorous and private exertion, and scourgings on my shins and underarms with inky grips of pumice. But the final step per Jillian Carbess's instructions—the clincher to bail out my sinking ship—that's the preparation of a familiar dish.

Entertaining tonite, the menu will be limited—Fauve is vegan, gluten-free, agonistic to the cruciferous, deathly allergic to onion, evasive of the deep burnt-umber of paprika and sweet potatoes, and gassy vis-à-vis beets.

Fauve delivers requests to me on the balcony. Her word, requests. The plates have been cleaned of the sautéed aubergine, wilted spinach and radicchio, and our empty tumblers set aside. We smoke, Fauve nuzzled into my lap, sharing the lone wicker chair. Headlight paces the balcony railing, indicating that the pillager of Beachwood—a brawny possum we've named Ultimo—has returned to terrorize the neighborhood.

Of Headlight's discomfiting ease with edges, and on this balcony of all places, she and I will talk later.

I have a request, Fauve says.

It's taken her a while for the usual orders of business. She has risen, raking Headlight's neck, back, and haunch. Her hair today is platinum. Costume bangles clink across her forearms. Her dress, a stiff 1960s shift, is printed with a single oversized monochrome daisy, split in the middle, black and white.

From her handbag, Fauve produces a collection of vellum and hands it over all-consequence, like she's relinquishing the deed to Monticello. On the first page is an embossed seal—an open hand, palm facing outward. The second page contains instructions in fine script. Slipping from my fingers before the gin-haze clears, the parchment glides beneath my chair. I stoop to retrieve it.

Backlit, body leaning against the wooden railing, Fauve's bouffant collars her shoulders. I drop the pages again. She is a visage of queendom, simmering and archaic. She extends her hand, coiled in rings, tracing first the bridge of my nose. A pause on the scarred cleft of my upper lip. Then a finger dips into my mouth. Gracious suzerainty, I grip her hand and pledge. To her shoes. Her patellas. Her subscapularis, clavicles, and to her left elbow on which my hand now rests—a weapon of war—a medieval mace, knobby and bulged.

∞ ∞ ∞

Whereas her typical requests supplied a driver and vehicle, Fauve of the Mouth's instructions were unspecific save my destination—Ojai—but contained such an excessive honorarium that I booked passage from Long Beach Harbor to nearby Port Hueneme in style via a small yacht, chartered out of Orange County, named *License to Chill.* For the remaining leg to Ojai, I would rent a car, or take a cab, or if this state of unusual magnanimity persists, try my thumb at hitch.

Headlight, I left behind, confined to our treehouse, rationed sufficiently, and counseled to aggravation. You may glide your hand across the back of your cat, and after that, you can only pray you've raised them right.

∞ ∞ ∞

Although the captain was generous with his beer, and though his well-scrubbed vessel featured a small built-in waterslide curling from a raised platform, I took to my cabin as the sun set for a moment of reflection. Not long after I descended, however, a disruption provoked me to return above board. *License to Chill's* captain, a futures trader, and his man, an intern who had previously spent our voyage trolling for halibut, stood armed now with a badminton racquet and a foldable beach chair, respectively. A second vessel drew along our starboard side.

The exchange between the two crafts was quite short. Beset as we were by a merciless volley of Roman candles and apocalyptic discharges from a flare gun, the captain retreated below deck, locking the trapdoor behind him. His man, cowering beneath an overturned bait chest, incapacitated from severe burns to the thigh, blubbered the superiorities of our captain's alma mater. As for me, I made the poor choice of ascending the ladder to the platform equipped with the waterslide, which exposed me to a barrage of direct fire from our adversaries.

Afforded only two options—immolation or drowning—I dove headfirst into the waterslide for a speedy denouement from our ship. Dismayed, for I avoid a public soak at all costs, I treaded water in the cold of the Pacific and there witnessed the captain of the enemy's vessel raise the spent cardboard shells of his Roman candles as dual scepters, sovereign of this smoldering world. He began a victory chant, soon joined by his compatriots: *Cornell, Cornell, Cornell, Big Red!*

I share an emotional affinity with the advance and retreat of tides. I gave in to their lull and appreciated the moon a—whitish-color— her stony imperfections and surrounding stars like unremovable stains, until the ships became distant specs and I washed ashore. I had booked passage with *License to Chill* to a port near Ventura. However, upon inquiring at a late-night beachside snack cabana, I found myself returned to familiar terra firma and only a short cab ride home to Beachwood Canyon, to Headlight.

Fauve of the Mouth had requested a measure of tact, discreteness, and professional affectation. I shaved before renewing her summons to Ojai, this time in my car, with my reliable leather portmanteau, The Old Man, and the freshly-cuddled Headlight, curled in the front seat.

We beat the dawn, breaching Ventura County while the sun was still a bashful yolk cracking east of the Topatopas.

Fauve of the Mouth's request concerned the resurfacing of an elusive counterpart in my profession—a man named de Guy—on the rooftops of Thomas Aquinas College. An emergence of interest to Fauve's handlers, who contracted me periodically. In addition to the formal instructions in the vellum, Fauve of the Mouth issued an individuated and strictly verbal command for me, her confidant—that Professor Donald Klineman, an endowed chair of classics at Thomas Aquinas, must be humbled.

Klineman's work I know from personal interest. Scholarship on his most recent text, *Magnets & Madrigals,* suggests the professor's thought has taken an obsessive turn towards which elements in consciousness may serve as the "Ground" to reorient rogue-dispositions of the Profane, Murderous, Taboo, and Sinister into harmonious Counterpoint. A curious evolution as legacy concerns of Klineman's project emphasize an inherent and radical indeterminacy, discussed under the heading "The Deviant Shadow," a subterfugic fixture of cognizance undoing the higher efforts of our most magnanimous madrigal selves.

In consulting The Old Man, I found my copy of *Magnets & Madrigals.* Pending the success of the Fauve Confrontation, I hope to secure Professor Klineman's autograph. On a personal note, I also intend to pressure Professor Klineman's call-to-arms—found in the pages of *De Rerum Canetis,* 6:8 (2001): 81-96. Print.—for the translation and recording of late-16th to early-17th century Italian madrigals into English. Klineman's efforts to stave off the extinction of the historical madrigal by increasing its contemporary exposure may produce a bloom of laymen bustle, but in their making will introduce to the world only sonic abominations.

But before any auditorium lectures from Professor Klineman, before any autographs, I must first see to the elusive agent, de Guy.

∞ ∞ ∞

Nothing. Nothing on the rooftops of Thomas Aquinas. Nothing here but bear shit, spider shit, lowse shit, bird shit, fox shit, ape shit, satyr shit, horse shit, fish shit, worm shit, immaterial shit, fly shit, ant shit, gyant shit.

∞ ∞ ∞

I sought out the esteemed lecturer instead. I found Professor Klineman in his office gathering materials amongst a group of flunkies whose own madrigal selves were diminished beyond repair.

In one hand, I carried my handsome portmanteau, The Old Man, from whose unclasped primary pocket Headlight's grey ears peeked. In the other, I held Klineman's book. Unable to privately dress down the Professor for those offenses heaped upon Fauve of the Mouth, I simply introduced myself by extending the text. The office-hours sycophants parted for this breach, at first passing the book amongst themselves towards Klineman, until a portly undergraduate with uncomfortably bushy sideburns cracked the text, paused upon my abundant marginalia for an intrusive moment, and thereafter tossed the book to his comrade, who alley-ooped it in a fluttering arc towards his man by the filing cabinet, who then lobbed the volume with deliberate intent toward the wastebasket in the corner.

This trajectory crossed the reach of Klineman, who rescued the book midflight, thumbed familiarly to the table of contents, and with a novelty pen from White Sands National Monument and an expression I can only describe as hope, dispensed a brief inscription.

∞ ∞ ∞

Locating Klineman's RV took me the better part of the professor's afternoon lecture. I had tried to attend this, truth be known, but the office hours sycophants barred my entrance at the door in a pose not unlike a line of scrimmage.

Parked in the student lot, the dusty Tioga bore the recognizable vanity plates from the Polaroid Fauve had given me—an embossed desert landscape and the letters NM PRDS. Querying The Old Man, I selected the Slim Jim and made quick work of the passenger door. The effects of the previous night at sea having diminished my stamina, I stowed away in the back bedroom atop a coarse rose-printed bedspread and soon fell asleep. And thusly deposed, I failed to notice my rumbling departure from Ojai.

∞ ∞ ∞

II

I HAVE THE LEATHERY VIGILANCE OF THE OLD MAN to thank for waking me before I was detected—he slid off the built-in shelving and released the cooped-up Headlight onto my face. NM PRDS appeared to be in mid-careen from the juncture of another highway spilling into the 101. Finding my sea legs, I cracked the brown accordion door of the RV's master bedroom. But whereas I expected Klineman, instead I found the four adulating youths from the professor's office performing a fraternal ritual in which shirts were tied around their necks, frosh love handles spilling over overtightened board shorts. Worse, on the built-in dining table, an arm wrestling contest had commenced for all those but the one with the bushy sideburns, for it was he who drove, his ineptitude at piloting a vehicle of this size causing those empty wine cooler bottles, raided from Klineman's personal stash, the most popular of which appeared to be Fuzzy Navel, to swerve with clanging equanimity from starboard to port and back again. I retreated to the closet to wait out the storm and slip away on calmer seas.

∞ ∞ ∞

But approaching hour three, sequestered in the closet, the gas tank of Klineman's RV apparently inexhaustible, I waited still, passing the time in examination of a shoebox of novelty souvenir vials stopped with small pieces of cork and stained with barbecue sauce. The Old Man rested between my feet. Headlight perched alternately on my head, shoulders, head. Stubble bloomed on my face, and with no recourse to manage my pulsing thereins and shave, it could only be endured.

The sun had set, but not before I had further opportunity, illumined by a sliver of light piercing into the cracked closet, to again digest Klineman's dedication in my copy of *Magnets & Madrigals:*

Reader,

The Deviant Shadow—already dated. Eastward motion, I am pending...none of the ocean, all of De Guise!

Sincerely,
  D. Klineman

PS—Aesthetically, I am in agreement with you about the madrigals.

The RV appeared to be slowing. I stole out of the closet and peeked through the blinds and could only presume we paused our venture so the undergraduates could visit a certain approaching roadside pornography emporium, which harkened passersby with an enormous electric neon sign of a buxom cowgirl in scanty western wear, firing off six-shooters. Over the marquis, the establishment's name flickered: "S_ippy McGo_ers Ho_se of C_ot"

Over the course of my professional career, I have found The Old Man to be a most reliable resource in situations such as these. In consultation with him, I selected the truncheon, the razor, and the small bar of soap, and prepared to make my stand.

∞ ∞ ∞

I sustained a few nicks and dings in the scuffle. I was, afterall, outnumbered four to one. But I had the element of surprise. And also the element of balance, for I had not compromised my sobriety so carelessly with so many wine coolers. To the first blond head, I descended a *thwack,* announcing my intent. And to the shoulders and legs of the second, something like a *thunk,* which communicated the business I meant. However, perceiving that the third undergraduate, who was the largest, though not the meanest, may succeed in doing me some harm, I immediately feinted a muscle spasm in my calf and collapsed to the floor near some of the poorly constructed cabinetry. And this purchased a crucial moment, for when the third approached me with his special brand of freshman schadenfreude, I clobbered his bare toes with the truncheon, then his arm, knuckles, chin, and back. Three down, one remained.

Our fearless captain, the driver, had just now returned from the Hose of Cot with the joyous report of legitimate nudity and steaks at $2.99. Comprehending the chaotic scene before him, he immediately turned to flee, perhaps to the protective bosom of the road sign. This retreat I halted with the descent of my truncheon, which collapsed the ringleader to the gravel like a song lingered too long on the Billboards.

The opportunity to perform for these undergraduates the deft work of a close shave—lather, strop, scrape, and rinse—upon the grotesquely unmanaged sideburns of the driver was a task I performed with diligence and delight. And with a final burst of inspiration, I improved on the driver's lightly-dreaded surfer mop by giving him a monk's tonsure.

Bound by their belts, still shirtless, back-to-back in a badly-tanned and bulging triad not dissimilar to Challah bread, I took care to sufficiently explain the benefits of the razor to the other squirming plebes. After shearing each in turn, I expelled the cohort behind a pottery shop near the city limits of Blythe and took the captain's chair of NM PRDS.

∞ ∞ ∞

There may be something to the vials in the RV's closet. Driving in to Doña Ana County, I discovered a series of self-made recordings by Professor Klineman in the center console of the RV—audio notebooks on cassette not yet catalogued in my bibliography. Any respectable scholarly distance from the Professor's unpublished ideas was overthrown by the unbecoming eagerness with which I thrust the first cassette into the tape deck.

After a delightful musical introduction—it is a well-known and guarded fact amongst his most devoted that Dr. Klineman frequently tours the secluded woodsy inns of the Eastern Seaboard under the pseudonym "Fender Rosinante," playing cover songs of the Laurel Canyon folk set for the guests on a small Spanish classical guitar— the professor's emotive baritone turned to speech:

> "In September of 1992, Mr. J.M. McGee, alias 'Slim Jim,' alias 'Jimmy the Fish,' alias 'The Javelina,' had traversed the lion's share of his boyhood fantasies and returned finally to San Acacia, New Mexico, to the home and booming BBQ business of his dear Aunt Marjorie.

> In the self-published memoir penned shortly before his disappearance, J.M. McGee recounted how a small band of his aunt's employees welcomed him back to New Mexico with a parade of pickup trucks, each dignified with the crest of the family restaurant, TEJAS BBQ—two longhorns eye-to-eye, pointed horns locked above their heads, and underneath, a single five pointed gold star atop a tower.

> The General Manager—Aunt Marjorie's lieutenant at TEJAS— greeted McGee like the prodigal nephew he was and decked him out in todo in a signature prophylactic TEJAS BBQ poncho that stretched to the tips of his boots and then set upon his head a kingsized collapsible sheriff hat generally reserved for youngsters' birthday parties. McGee knew then that all was forgiven, for this costume indicated the game that all offroading New Mexicans with a four wheel drive vehicle and access to a cooking pit play:

they would race the badlands. And along the way, they would *Bump & BBQ*.

General Manager put McGee in the middle seat of his truck and called first pick. From over in a lineup of employees, he summoned a pockmarked chickenshit in dungarees to drive their truck. This with a wink at McGee.

As the trucks exited the airport onto those rarely traversed New Mexico backroads, it seems a passage into boyhood, and those deviances of southwestern adolescence began afresh.

Rattling around in the cab, GM wasted no time in distributing charred pieces of spatchcocked chicken, hot links, and hunks of brisket from a large clay warmer between his feet. As for their driver, GM stuck a long, fatty beef rib in his fixed mouth, and the driver held it there like a pro bird dog, nary a nibble.

Soon, they'd outrun the other trucks and shifted to a coast. Only when the stragglers finally crested in the sideview mirrors did their driver kick pedal into a wide and skidding donut. McGee lost his grip on a quart of Q-juice, and it drenched the cab like they rode with the Ripper.

'Not once in my life,' J.M. McGee wrote in that memoir, 'had I *Bumped and BBQ'ed* better than that evening, sticky to swarm the bees, riding on that boy's intuition to Aunt Marjorie's hidden pits where her best work is done. And just like my young years, I saw the sun give it up like a big-ass glowing frisbee over that everlasting barren white sand-wash. I knew then my next phase of living. I'd soon take the reins of TEJAS. I'd rev it. And all I needed was the right partners.'

When the tapes ended, I drove for several hours in silence, stopping for gas on the cash reserves of The Old Man. And I was mystified. What divergent interests for Professor Klineman, so usually steeped in historical and sonic minutae. The aliases; the attention given to the memoir of an apparent bad actor. I confess, I found the whole thing as irresistible as a bad spy novel, complicated by a near spiritual hunger for pulled pork. The nearest TEJAS BBQ was in Thoreau, but a grandmother with two babes on her hips at the gas station suggested I see the original TEJAS location further south on 1-25.

Klineman's recounting of his own pilgrimage to San Acacia on cassette tape #2, warblier and palimpsested over his original folk ballads, solidified this direction...

"My scenic route to San Acacia seeking the origins of TEJAS BBQ took me past The Valencia County Detention Center and a short while later, The New Mexico Corrections Department, a boxy white building with two floors surrounded by the customary barbwire. Nearing nine in the morning, I reached the architectural signs of a city. But even drawing towards the town square, not a soul showed itself. On the previous occasion I had visited, I spent a pleasant day followed by two frisky and uncollared Blue Heelers who must have escaped from their yard, and similar to this spirit, I seemed to remember a kind of bubbly excitement amongst the residents concerning rumors of the construction of a summertime waterpark that would offer travelers reason to pause, perhaps for the duration of a long holiday weekend, in this humble city rather than commit to the slightly more glamorous Los Lunas or a push on towards nearby Socorro. Recalling this communal buoyancy, it alarmed me that San Acacia could have so rapidly degenerated into the dust bowl before me. Of course, I realize now, the town's succumb to economic decrepitude must have been unavoidable given the political inevitabilities of the 1980s, especially surrounding the election of Sam Giancaca as Mayor, a campaign coinciding with my first visit to San Acacia, when city council meetings were held and samples of the bulbous blue plastic tubing that would one day be fitted into steep, fast waterslides and the sizable artificial panels that would frame a basin for a state of the art tidepool, were trotted out and praised by Giancaca as the cure for the deadly disease of economics. These developments could only have produced amongst the townsfolk bona fide hope their fates could change for the better, a hope that was earnestly escalated by the expansion of San Acacia' success story and native daughter, Marjorie McGee, til in time those expectations imploded by an overextension of resources, natural disasters, and all the usual scandals related to corrupt city administration. San Acacia's fall from prosperity was swift and merciless. The plans for the water park, taped proudly to the inner window of the city planner on a Main Street of sorts, were discarded. A flash flood caused by the sudden rising of poorly monitored tributaries uprooted a number of generational households, sending those residents to nearby Bernardo. The primary street grew besotted with boarded shop doors, broken windows, back entrances kicked in, and the structures raided. *For Sale* signs went unanswered so long they bleached to an ephemeral yellow haze, their posts splintering in the desert sun. Residents who remained witnessed the clientele of their businesses dry up, and with their fingertips sliding against the mountain face of perpetual arrears, had finally eaten sand. Whereas there had once stood a tailor, an independent bookstore, a women's social club, a penny arcade, a Golden Corral buffet, a pet store, a record shop, a feed supply, a barber, a general physician's office, a community grocer's market, and an architect, behind whose office a ravenous coyote now skittered, each of these landmarks of burgeoning affluence I'd witnessed on my visit before were gone.

And so on this day I followed instead that boned and hungry predator, pillaging for scraps behind the city planner's destitute office, and in the coyote's scavenging wake, ascended a set of dissolving cement steps to peer into a dumpster filled with all manner of construction debris. Here I found an attaché case containing blueprints for the expected waterpark, a boutique motel, and TEJAS BBQ #17."

∞ ∞ ∞

III

PARKED DISCREETLY BEHIND A SAFEWAY, I searched the closets and undercarriage of Klineman's Tioga. In the latter, I found the attaché he'd mentioned on cassette tape #2, and inside, the blueprints. Drawing up a chair, I poured a tall glass of ice water, working late into the night to assemble the schema not of TEJAS, but of the waterpark, enticed especially by the light-penciled rendering of a peculiar building that would house an Olympic-sized swimming pool. From the center of the pool, a doublewide curving staircase extended to the ceiling, then, through a hole cut through the roof, ended in separate platform thirty feet into the sky. This aerial stage was encased in clear, thick, secure plastic, affording a view of the mostly flat San Acacian landscape. A large green tube exited the transparent box, and beginning at the platform, looped, dropped swiftly, and snaked again around the exterior before dumping the slippery passenger back into a far corner of the pool, set apart by nets and buoys.

Headlight pawed at the piece of tape securing the corner at the upper right blueprint, licked the adhesive, grew bored, began batting again, sprawling, crinkling the paper. I rubbed my eyes, on hour two here; Headlight upset Klineman's drafting tools; four hours now, 3am; an eye on The Old Man, Headlight sprawled and preened, drifting to bored, eyes drifting off, mine too, shutting, again, sprawl, again...

> The afternoon the rules of science were overturned, I was early for an appointment at a New Mexico salon. From the chair, I wafted. In front of me hovered a glossy magazine of popular but absurd hairstyles. I gripped the magazine, let it go, and still it lingered. Stylists regarded their separation from the tile. Distracted by a group of somersaulting polish bottles, a manicurist cried out as a curling iron tethered to the outlet burned her thigh.

Closest to the salon door, I opened it as the foundations of the shopping center separated from the earth. Everything was rising: trees disentangled from the soil; telephone poles strained against their connecting wires. Restaurant linens drifted like specters around pool tables, tumbleweeds, lawn furniture.

The city disembarking went forth, and all our detritus went with it.

There were the Pans, who took advantage of gravity's absence and tried swimming. Others, palsied from shock, simply floated among the debris. I pushed off a stroller to a slowly spinning recreational vehicle. Leveraging against the rear tire, I aimed for a café table a few feet below. A beachball below that. A vending machine below that.

I would see Fauve of the Mouth, see Ojai again, before we drifted past oxygen.

Settling into a westwind, I rested on a billboard, then in modified leapfrog, began my cross of the desert. An elderly woman and her two leashed canines I fended off with a crowbar.

Little colonies erupted around this provisioned house or that until, depleted of supplies, they fell into infighting and brutality.

I suffered migraines. Caskets, in their slow rotation, unhinged, spilling their contents to the sky. Once—on a still-fleshed corpse—I was forced to maneuver.

A man, Ros Scorcier, found me in the sky above the Inland Empire. He rode on a bicycle fashioned with foot levers and pulleys. Connected to his hand controls, sails paired with slatted resisters allowed for downward progress as the trilling of his fingers caused them to unfold and rearrange.

Ros aided me, he said, because I would have perished in Windmill Valley without him. This was the swan song in a life of good deeds before he pedaled past the coastline to examine those behemoths of the sea he expected had surfaced. What would happen, I asked, when he grew so tired he could no longer pedal? To which he reminded me we could not topple over.

Harnessed in Ros' sidecar, for the first time in two hundred miles, I fell deeply into sleep

> ...my treehouse in Beachwood, Fauve of the Mouth in a simple, flowing white gown. Music plays. Every time an A# is struck, mice squeak. Fauve of the Mouth sashays down Franklin on foot, striking mute those watching. We leap the crosswalks, playing.
>
> Simon Says, run the gauntlet, stage a play, eat the evidence. Simon Says, kill your uncle, split the difference, flip a coin.
>
> I am in an arena. In the first cage, Fauve of the Mouth sits with Headlight, stroking her fur. In turn, Headlight licks the sweat from the webs of Fauve's other hand with a coarse, dehydrated tongue.
>
> In another cage, Fauve of the Mouth discusses the Klineman Affair with two worthy brass bells and a wild boar, who sits opposite her at the table.
>
> In a third cage, she receives from her handlers the vellum. Her hair is wet, slicked back. The cover bears the initials DG...

For three weeks I've ridden in this aircraft. Ros constructs a reserve tank of drinking water thanks to the abundance of plastic bottles from a grocery store. I have fashioned a harpoon to spear animals, both those recently perished but not yet rotting, and those living and maddened, drawing them in to cleave, skin, mince, then roast upon a trailing sterno campstove. We now have two linked bicycles, the construction of which required a remarkable feat of cooperation and acrobatics. And between the two bicycles we have built a conjoining basin secured with a lid of thinly meshed chicken wire for the archival preservation of papers and small objects. The optimist in Ros cannot say no to paraphernalia.

Our agreement is we will separate once we have reached the coast. But at the sight of a shorn sign for Dana Point Harbor, Ros blubbers a bit and offers to stay on for the long haul. Our rations have been replenished—we've added a collection of long rifles, a fog machine for diversion, scraps of long johns shredded and woven into a flag, and put to use a batch of watercolors on the flanks of the airship. The possibilities for preservation are preserved. And so we turn northwards together, towards Fauve of the Mouth.

Near what must be Laguna Beach, Ros spies a soothsayer in the distance with his looking glass.

The man is bound by ropes, wrapped around his torso, to a dozen birdmen who encircle him. Strapped to the birdmen's arms and legs are miscellany and fuselage: plastic siding, laminated political yard signs, motorcycle bugshields, and sheets rigged to catch the breezes. Several of the birdmen appear at rest while the others maintain the coterie by flapping vigorously to lower the group back towards the surface.

The soothsayer presides over a barrel fastened to his body, marked with a yellow HAZMAT symbol, which he cracks open in a sacred ritual. From a stainless steel ladle, he drinks deeply. Drawing the birdmen hand-over-hand towards the barrel, the soothsayer performs this sacrament for each in turn. The men, at the moment of imbibing, slump over. But after a brief stupor, revivified, they turn towards our airship with a frightful beating of wings.

Prepare for me the Kentucky long rifles, Ros orders. To which I ready the quick charges, powder the first barrel, and load the minie ball. Securing half cock, I pass the rifle to Ros who braces the long black barrel into the crooked-Y of a tripod. I begin provisioning the second rifle.

Ros proposes a game—we have approximately six shots before we are reached. He produces an antique coin from the collection in which we found the rifles. Heads, the prophet, Tails, the barrel, Ros suggests. He flips. Heads. He shoots, missing the prophet by a wide margin. A worthy shot, I say. He flips. Again, Heads. He fires the second rifle, this time eliminating the arm of one of the birdmen. I have re-loaded the first piece. Ros flips...Heads, a third time. The prophet shields himself with the bleeding birdman, who receives the ball full in the chest. Cut free, the birdman floats to the side, his wound seeping into the air. Ros flips again. Heads. This is quite unusual, he says. He aims at the prophet's rotted mouth, fires. But the rifle jams. He flips again, Heads, the prophet is close enough now to lob a ladle of waste, more for menacing impression than physical damage, the green viscous substance traveling but six feet or so, stalling, and beginning to float upward. Ros fires, removing from the prophet his left leg from the knee downward. One of the birdmen hastens and grips the severed limb by the ankle, wielding it as a club. I pass the final rifle to Ros, who flips.

Heads.

I prepare for hand to hand combat, arming myself with a blunted practice rapier. Ros aims for the prophet's heart. We have gained an immense amount of altitude and he is lightheaded. He fires, and his shot is low and to the left, striking instead the barrel of waste. A metallic spark. The explosion bathes the birdmen in an eruption of green, blood, and flame.

We go on. Somewhere near Salinas, extreme crosswinds circled the drifting remains of a business specializing in professional document shredding. The papercuts from that force majeure are excruciating, yet, Ros, standing in his seat and bound by his ankle straps, extends his swimming pool skimmer on a telescopic pole, netting batch after batch of the chattel. I manage our craft away from the cyclone, and on clearer skies we begin our usual procedure of sorting the collection. The bulk of it is junk mail or has already fallen to the work of the shredder. But a number of acquisitions—whole documents bound with twine—are secure and they bear a series of rose-blossom kisses; the unmistakable imprint of Fauve of the Mouth.

These, look here, Ros shows me, raising the documents in each hand above his head. These missives are for me alone. They carry the markings of my love, Fauve of the Envelope.

∞ ∞ ∞

The Old Man woke me, falling off the desk. The Tioga shook on its shocks like a California quake.

Fauve of the Envelope?

Clearly under siege, I reached inside The Old Man for the Kentucky long rifles. But he provided me instead with the truncheon. A window in the back bedroom shattered, and I rushed to it, delivering a blow to the infiltrating bald head. In tandem, Headlight commenced a ferocious scratching.

Preparing for my final stand, I was hauled off my feet from behind, lifted into the air, and suplexed atop the rose bedspread, then pinned without recourse under a blubbery dogpile.

∞ ∞ ∞

IV

I WISH TO LIVE FACTS. EPISTEMIC CORRECTNESS is the baseline for eudaemonia. Though knocked unconscious and bound, I believe I have been stuffed in the storage compartment underneath the master bed in the RV's rear bedroom. The Old Man I feel beside me, unable to advise. Headlight mews, but the sound is muted.

I am tortured through radio bossanova, an entire episode of Coast to Coast dedicated to a cult of projectionauts, and the undergraduates' acapella mutilations of classic madrigals. At least I am able to check the state of my thereins and have the opportunity for a measure of reflection.

There is Fauve's request to find de Guy that began this caper. There are the henchman undergraduates to whom I owe this roughhousing. And spanning the nature of "which Fauve is it?"—The Mouth? The Envelope?—is the Klineman Affair—a messy audio rendering of the esteemed Doc's preoccuptation with J.M. McGee and the burgeoning of a New Mexico BBQ dynasty.

I gather from Headlight's strangled cries we could be approaching Yuma. I can only strain against my bonds. And when they finally break like dessicated leather, I open my notebook and pass the time as I do on occasion in imagination and fancy, penning a short work of prose loosely inspired by lore, recent events, and flashes of inspiration under my pen name, "Templeman."

The Saga of Aquifer & Sal Giancana: A Story of Love, Loss, and Fins
By Templeman

I met him in a bar in Ojai. He was a man with a haunted look in his eye, a man who'd made a lot of mistakes.

"What are you drinking, stranger?" I asked.

"Fernet Branca, one cube of ice," he muttered.

I nodded to the barkeep and ordered him up another. The man looked at me with curiosity, and that's when I noticed he was cupping a bell in his hands.

"You're probably wondering about this bell? It's made from alchemical silver," he said.

The barkeep set the Fernet in front of it, and he swallowed it down in one gulp.

"I'm a detective," he said. "I have a house not too far from here. And a deck in the back. Used to sit on it with a girl in a tulip dress. See, there are girls like Thelma, and there are girls like Tulip-Dress. Any old timer will tell you a Thelma is worth a thousand Tulip-Dresses, but we never figure that out until it's too late, do we?" Suddenly he looked down at his bell and asked, "do you know anything about the Silver Forest?"

"No," I said, deeply regretting my decision to strike up a conversation with a stranger.

That's when he decided to tell me a story. And since I am conflict-avoidant and had nowhere specific to be, I sat there and listened.

"I once knew a girl named Aquifer," he said. "She was different from most girls you meet these days—about seventy percent more aquatic. She got into trouble with an organization called Avalanche. Perhaps you've heard of it. It's a cult of sorts, or a gathering of like-minded individuals, as they would put it. See, she'd taken a trip away from her mermaid sisters—the Madri Gals, perhaps you've heard of them—and while she was on her jaunt, Avalanche got its claws into her. They drew her in with promises of astral projection, wayward magic, and dresses made from spun silver and gold. Aquifer, always was a sucker for a good dress. Now, I imagine you'll think this all is a bunch of hooey [our detective narrator was three sheets to the wind at this point, and given to using words like hooey], and I'm apt to agree with you, except where it comes to astral projection. I myself met a guy who could do it, or who will be able to do it once he procures the proper tools—knowledge, of course, being chief among these. Now, at Avalanche, Aquifer counted herself one of the faithful, but one night she realized she missed her sisters, and that her true calling was performing underwater mermaid spectacles with them, because when underwater mermaid spectacles are one's true calling, really nothing else will suffice. They don't say you can't keep a good girl from her fins for nothing. So, one night she broke out of Avalanche and made her way back to her home, back to the Madri-Gals. Now, the Madri-Gals were something to see. Let me tell you. They had an underwater mermaid extravaganza, and they were popular. On a typical Summer Saturday, they'd play three packed shows. And it was such a Saturday when Aquifer returned home, but when she got there, she found the grounds deserted, the house empty, and worst of all, the mermaid grotto completely drained.

"Aquifer was at a loss, and beside herself with grief, so she did what any right-thinking person would do. She hired the best detective she could to find her sisters. And that man was Sal Giancana. She met him at his dimly lit office, light from the streetlamp across the way trickling through the blinds like fat stripes in bacon. She walked into that office in her high heels and fishnet stockings hoping to look like a femme fatale but feeling every bit the little mermaid at heart.

"When he saw her, Giancana stubbed out his cigarette and let out a long, low whistle. He said all the appropriate things a detective like him ought to say to a slip of a fish like Aquifer. He even called her dame, and before she could say "would you look at that; I think I've got a run in my stocking," she'd lost her heart to this potent gumshoe with his larger-than-average firearm. She hired him straight away but decided there would be no second base until he'd solved the case.

"Giancana got to work, and it wasn't long before he had a lead. A priest wearing headphones who called himself "the Chaplain" led him straight to an organization called the Tower. Aquifer had heard of the Tower. She wasn't certain what they did, but she knew among the people of Avalanche that there were whispers. The Tower, it seemed, had forged literature to sway opinion that Avalanche was a cult instead of a religious organization and Avalanche had retaliated by fabricating paperwork to have the Tower listed as a cult instead of whatever it was the Tower claimed to be for tax purposes. Soon they were both caught in an ouroboros of red tape, and metaphorical shots were fired. But Giancana was a man of action, much more interested in actual shots fired, and in possession of a near phobia where any paperwork was concerned. So instead of going through any of the relevant forms, he followed a woman named Thelma, an agent of the Tower—and the sweetest damn gal this side of the Mississippi—until he located a detective on their payroll. Now," the man said, gripping his refreshed Fernet Branca and fixing his gaze on me. "Who do you think that detective was?"

"I think it was you," I said.

"Sharp as a tack, my boy. That's right. It was me. Giancana caught up with me at an art museum called The Cranefly. I wasn't there on a case. I was simply perusing, gaining some culture. I clocked the guy right away and drew my weapon. He drew his, and I jumped behind a bench. He darted behind a sculpture of a Spanish galleon, pistol at the ready. I took a shot, clipping off the tip of the foremast. He executed a phenomenal dive-roll, weaving between elderly patrons' legs—geriatric grande dames refusing to give up their day at the museum, even at risk of death. He slipped completely out of sight after that, and though I searched the museum, I wouldn't come into contact with him again until three nights later when I awoke from a gentle slumber to see his imposing figure standing over me, gun in hand, fedora tipped over an eye. He said, 'You and me, we're going to talk, see.'"

"And with a line like that, I must say, I was given to disclosure. We went out on my deck and had a few beers. I gave him the details he wanted, and he went on his way. Before he left, though, I stole all the cash out of his wallet. He never knew. Later that month, I received an envelope from him. It seemed he'd managed to rescue the Madri-Gals from certain death (a rescue performed at the apex of a high-speed roller coaster, no less). The Madri-Gals, it turned out, were a front for a nefarious cult (which one, I never learned), and the girls were all safe, but had been placed in witness protection. He and Aquifer were married at the girls' new place of business, and a little mer-bundle was one its way courtesy of the stork. He included a photo of the two of them dressed in bridal gear. They were beaming, and surrounded by Aquifer's sisters, all of them lined up in costume at the new waterpark. As part of their compliance with witness protection they'd altered the colors of their sparkly tails, and I could see from the banner they stood beneath that they'd changed their names (inexplicably) to the Spinning Platter Fishes."

The detective set down his drink and showed me the photo. On the back was written: Aquifer and Sal Giancana, 1954.

I had no idea why he was telling me any of this. I didn't care about mermaid girls, or Sal Giancana. The bell, though, that had captured my fancy.

"How much for the bell?"

"Not for sale," he said grimly.

"Then what's it for?"

"Hell if I know. I just do what they tell me. And the bells, see, they're all part of it. That's how they get you." He took a sip of his drink. "Do you know anything about Dutch alchemists?"

I was starting to look for the exit. "I can't say that I do, no."

He seemed annoyed. "Then do you know anything about astral projection?"

"No."

He looked around suspiciously at the other patrons.

"Sometimes do you feel like someone's watching us? Someone tired and sweaty and waiting at a mechanic's office for his car to be fixed?"

"You're losing me," I said. I had to get away from this guy, but I had a single lingering question. "The money, did you ever return it to Giancana?"

He turned away and stared deep into his drink like the love of his life was lost somewhere deep inside it. "No," he whispered.

"Even after he sent you that wedding photo?" I said, my disappointment audible.

He shook his head slowly. "Kid, there are things I've done that I'm not proud of, but sometimes you need to know when to call it a day…

V

IT WASN'T FOR REAL, FAUVE SAYS. Her arms are around Klineman's neck. A leg, extending from her skirt, lifts to an acute triangle, and an inky pump dangles from her toes.

I knew you loved his research. I thought it'd be a great way to meet. We never thought you'd stowaway!

Breakfast concludes at Bonnie Lu's. Klineman takes the check. Full professor.

Almost 24 hours since the undergraduates expelled me at the edge of town and doubled back towards New Mexico on some research jaunt with Klineman's permission, an unasked question now sits with us at the table—whether, when this conciliatory breakfast club reaches the parking lot, Fauve will leave in my car or Klineman's. I am not in my best state.

Love, it's pure assignment. Fauve gets in Klineman's car.

Later that night, the Old Man gave me prim revelation; spilled out Klineman's book as I lay prostrate and dismantled on my treehouse's suicide balcony, filing experiences in the mental category: "Under What Delusion Do I Advance Myself A Professional to the World?"

There. There it is. In Klineman's own hand in his inscription in *Magnets & Madrigals:*

> *"none of the ocean, all of De Guise!"*

∞ ∞ ∞

VI

THE ENVELOPES AND THE PACKAGES BEGAN ARRIVING in my Beachwood mailbox the following day.

Thank you cards. Of sorts.

first,

> For services rendered, the Baroness extends the gratitude of the realm. Enclosed, find the requested sum alongside an additional gratuity. Your delicacy with respect to public acknowledgment of her errands, we trust, will exceed those professional courtesies thus far effected.

then,

> Greetings in Proportion to Your Iniquity,
>
> You have fulfilled your charge, that much we acknowledge. But not without parlous distress afflicted upon the townspeople of St. Augustine, equally substantial property damage, and most grievously, the matter of Ros & Ros's daughter, Headlice. An honorable man would not further the blight of illegitimation. Find enclosed your fee, but may an undiluted conscience dictate its application.

another,

> This has been a riot! Mea culpa, had to borrow a few bucks from your share. We'll settle up when we sell the rights. Lining up *Hollywood, Dateline, 60 Min*, now (not to mention all the new biz coming in). Yours in grassy knolls, etc.

The letters were accompanied by crates of dubloons, rupees, a molded loaf of banana bread, a brace of antique pistols, a lone denarius, a moneyclip of US fifties, selfshot erotic polaroids, a sort of strange triangular external hardrive without any recognizable method of connecting to a computer, luxurious pelts, a lone fish, and in its mouth a drachma.

This largesse, bizarre, thrilling at first, proved a terrible distraction, for Fauve arrived back at the treehouse, all apologies, reinforcing the integrity of her original missive and the charge to find de Guy, or had she said 'De Guise' all the while through her slight lisp, before the unintended Klineman debacle. For Fauve *had* been instructed by her handlers to retain me before my errant RV errand, she said, and so on, and more. She brought Japanese noodles. We ate on barstools in the kitchen.

The dense time-stop of sterling. The document from the British Constable, addressed from Whitechapel, concerning the successful detainment of Cliff Deering. Tributary of the small jade statue in the velvet bag.

The artifacts accumulated, filled the Old Man completely, then overran the guest room, crept beyond the French doors, and overtook the balcony. I covered the assemblage with tarps.

∞ ∞ ∞

I try to limit our calls, but when my thereins reach tidal waves, I ring Jillian Carbess in St. Louis, ring her in her chair. She is an elder stateswoman of my profession; a mentor of sorts.

I can't parse it, I say. Is it Fauve, Fauve of the Mouth, or Fauve of the Envelope?

The most important question, says Jillian...

Is what the hell am I supposed I do with this mélange?

I am pacing the newly erected shelving in the living room, categorizing incoming rarities. Return to Sender doesn't seem viable.

You wouldn't believe what I am holding, I tell her. A purse of rubles and heartfelt gratis for tying the loose ends on Dyatlov Pass. Do you want to know what happened?

Jillian is calm, measured as always. A saint to us sinners.

First, consider provenance, then providence, she says. The prizes could be real...could be earned. Darling, they could be yours.

de Guy? Know him? I ask. What about De Guise?

You know you can't ask me that.

How about J.M. McGee? TEJAS BBQ? Ring any bells?

Professional ethics bind me, she says.

But I'm one of the good guys, I say, my voice at a near-whine. Shamed, I set the phone down for pushups. Anything to pull this plane up.

That you are my darling. I swear a sigh pushes from the receiver.

Rolling onto my back, Headlight plops on my stomach. I reach back for the receiver.

Klineman? I ask. Is he off limits too?

Donald! Have you read his latest? It's good. Great even.

He signed my copy. My God, Jillian, I'm looking at a shelf with a rusty sabre that could fall off and shish kebab me. Or at least give me tetanus.

You know, she says, and the sound of nail file grating keratin fills the phone, Klineman rarely endorses his work. It may be worth something.

I'm overdone on rarities at the moment.

Listen, I'm due for another call. Let's continue in a day or two.

Please. Yes, please. I'll maintain the routine. Shave, exercise, rinse, cook.

It may be time to modify. You could consider gardening, or my thing, tea. And dear, if the treasures of antiquity are really, truly unwanted you have my forwarding address.

I need reinforcements, Jil. Bring a goodie bag.

∞ ∞ ∞

VII

DIMLY, AS IF IN A MIRROR, I see Fauve at the top of a black alabaster staircase.

The staircase is an ornately carved and sweeping thing, history longer than civilizations have crafted storm cellars, church steps, moving sidewalks. Under Fauve's feet, the steps are narrow, but closer to me, on the ground-floor, they widen past any ergonomic consideration. Twin banisters streak like fallen angels. Small injunctions of cloudy grey rupture the black expanse.

On the railing above every step hangs a dress on a uniform hanger. Framed placards label *The Fletched Arrow* and *Short Changed* at a *Hanging.* Midway between us rests Truth is in a Paperback Maple Tonight. Fauve places her hand down the rail, as far as she can reach, suspending her body across the staircase, straining towards a dress named *The Hotel Parmenides*, nearest to me on the final step.

The frame flickers. Like this effort never happened, Fauve is regal again, composed, on that top step. In her hands is a dress, sleeveless, black, and magnetic. The dress's name is *Octopus Ink.* She removes it from the hanger and steps into the dress, pulling the framed bodice over her hips and waist. She zips it herself. Tufts of crisp, latticed organza bloom around her clavicles.

Fauve of the Dress says, entertainment staves off the rest of life until the film catches fire and infringes on my moment. It is my moment. I take it with me in my clutch with popcorn and half a box of Raisinettes. It is my moment; my opportunity to come full circle. On every step I have a dress designed for my moments.

I turned away, just for a moment, and turn back in time to see her dive down the steps.

Her leap should bring her to the bottom of the staircase, to the last dress. But the staircase responds like a charging Egyptian warhorse, outbounding her to the final step. She appears to move in distance, but for every step she gains, the banisters remain just ahead of her.

She rises, hand slipping from the railing at the top of the staircase, *Octopus Ink* puddled beside her.

She speaks to the last dress, she reasons with it: my creature, threatened by an axiom, my creature, alone at the end of my actual infinite.

She curses the dress; she changes its name.

∞ ∞ ∞

VIII

ALL THAT MATTERS PERSISTS.

I take to downtown on foot, where an undergirding hope there flickers: for an event of value to materialize, enough to squelch my thereins.

An early lunch at a food cart led a series of promising experiences— the slight tension of my incisors against the membranous casing of a bacon-wrapped street dog—the burst of juice and pickled onion, heavily graced with mustard.

Strides to outrun my black dog bummers.

Thereafter, I observed the bickering chess match of two reclining savants on Skid Row, unable to hide my amusement at black's advance of a rook to F-6.

I may yet be saved.

Then, at a sidewalk gallery of spectacular quinceañera arrangements near the California Flower Mall, I succeeded in negotiating the discounted purchase of a day-old display, sizeable enough to require an easel, and with nary noticeable wilting of the bulging vibrant roses, calla lilies, and blush tulips.

Huzzah!

Spring in my step, I made the short walk to the nearby garment district to pay my respects to Raheem Tabash, a confidant who provided the charcoal gabardine, without the customary base charge for yardage minimums, for the made-to-measure suits I wear as a kind of uniform.

Raheem inspects my blazer, his hands automatically sizing up the shoulders, the lapel, probing at the elbows, patting down the arms. Finding me satisfactory, he kisses my face. In a flash, I worry my unshaved cheeks have chafed his pillowy jowls.

The walls of his office show safari photographs collaged alongside newspaper and magazine clippings from past clients of his fabric house who've made a splash. Outside his office windows, Raheem's assistants escort clients' assistants as they trim swatches and tour aisles of trendy rayon blends stacked a dozen feet tall.

Good to see you, my Mann! Raheem is jolly, but looking me over, his mood sombers. Hey, what is it? Same ol' shame hole?

A thought occurs; Raheem thumbs a stack of fashion magazines on his desk.

See this? he asks.

What's that?

Your lady friend, the one you brought to my Christmas party. Fi? Fe. Fay?...Fiona?

Fauve.

Sure, that's right; she's in the *Times*. This week! Couldn't miss her cheekbones.

Raheem slides the Style section of the paper across his desk. Lead on the runway, a line of arresting models behind her, Fauve wears a chartruese dress cut on the bias with a neckline near to her navel.

Raheem is beaming. It's De Guise's new collection, he says, the fabric sourced within these walls.

And over the next half hour, Raheem told of the formation of the empire of De Guise...

"Big story, something in here for everyone. Begins in Missouri at a family-owned-and-operated steel wool finishing factory. He's called Jaakko Sprawley, a Finnish boy, and he's languishing in the Midwest. The whole longing life, dreaming of peckers and Steve Carlton in uniform and dressing up in bedsheets to 'Rocketman' when he should be callousing up his hands reaping the family's harvests. So one windy April afternoon, he's playing hooky from work on the family property, and he's separated from his parents. What I mean is, when everyone else flees to the cellar because a tornado has come calling, he's not where he's supposed to be. So there in the yard, with his arms and legs coiled around the rough bark of a tree, a Flowering Dogwood, it's the laundry of his mother's on the clothesline when the tornado touched down that spurred Jaako's preternatural instinct with clothing. A tragic gift, but it carried instant enlightenment.

Grey death harkened near the house, and what I mean is the multiplicity of silhouette was here revealed to Jaako. Prophetically. The clothing strained against the clothespins, houndstooth and calico whipping about, and men's workwear too, probably Tennessee cotton, and his mother's many dresses, those poly-blends that dominated late-70's Sears, and pale underclothes in delicate lace, and baseball tees, faded thin. In the pandemonium of textile, Jaako witnessed trends for a thousand years, lightly damp, flaring and flattened, ballooning, cross-hatched, pastiched, flipped sidewise, and individualized to pin-prick thin, until a final surge of wind took the line and plucked the posts right from the ground. A celestial tumble cycle, ripped to the sky.

The finger of God landed. Came tapping on the door of the Sprawley cellar, caved it in, and took the family. Only Jaakko was spared, true as I tell you, wrapped around that Flowering Dogwood only a few dozen yards away.

Jaakko's father was tight. An admirable handle on the management side of things, and Jaakko was the only living heir. So, he's fifteen, inheritor of multiple life insurance policies and the profits of the business's assets, packed away into a trust, and then Jaako is sent off to an estranged aunt here in LA.

At first, Jaakko agonizes over the density of the city. But the tragedy affords him worldmaking beyond imagination. He was in the right place. The realization he is *this* kind of person sets in. Auntie, a bit eccentric, helps, too. Jaakko tells, for example, in the *Vanity Fair* profile, of her gifts over the next few birthdays: plastic Godzilla finger puppets with packaging in Japanese, a Talking Heads cassette, a military side bag, a year membership to the Silent Movie Theatre on Fairfax, a gas mask.

And then Jaakko meets Robin Schwartz at one of these underground punker clubs in the mid-8os. All those early photos you see of Jaakko, that's Robin hanging off his shoulder, or looking miserable somewhere in the background, mesh shirt, mohawked, whereas Jaakko had an affinity for a distressed houndstooth summer blazer rolled up over his elbows.

When Jaakko and Robin chat over their sartorial common ground and concoct some interest in developing a clothing line, Robin's father, a restaurateur, just absolutely desperate for any indication of an employable future in his kid, a likelihood seeming more cosmic by the minute, says sure, let me dump sixty thousand in here, set up my kid with an accountant and business manager and give him some rope to play a bit. See if we can't broker out some kind of future, if just enough to tip the scales. Of course, Jaako is independently wealthy here, but nobody really knows the extent of it. So, Jaakko goes in and matches the 6oK investment, and the youths are off to the races, dba SPRAWLING ROBIN.

The debut collection—this was F/W 1991—sputters out. Quality control, fabric printing errors, supply chain, nothing here to indicate endemic failure, just the usual hurdles. But Jaakko, don't count him out.

Because the whole time F/W '91 is on the ropes, Jaako is secretly working on a women's collection. A back room at the Spring Street warehouse is filled with dress forms and mannequins, bolts of fabric draped, tacked, windswept. So, when fresh off the heels of F/W '91 comes the real debacle of Spring/Summer '92, and Robin's father is one bad month's P&L away from pulling rescue funding, smart cookie Jaakko knows precisely when and how to maneuver. He axes the bespoke menswear stuff and unveils this covert prêt-à-porter women's direction, already with the samples prepped, and the preliminary fabric sourcing done right here in this building.

He called a spade a diamond—or more accurately, diamonds. Or more accurately, millions of diamonds. The collection is bats straight from production. IT-girls rocket fuel the brand on their own volition. A total deluge of press. Numbers to make a seasoned buyer salivate.

Robin, he's gunshy from the first round of setbacks. But sensing relief, and maybe a bit of fatherly approval, he sits back and moves with the current.

Then strange things begin to happen around SPRAWLING ROBIN, and Jaakko and Robin get concerned. Financial statements pour in from unrecognizable institutions. There's a thick manila folder of trademark paperwork. A sampling of unrequested swatches arrives from an overseas fabric house addressed to a partially obscured and unrecognizable name. Jaakko is on a research trip in Nice, and he gets a call from Robin that a woman Robin's never seen has dropped by with instructions for a mandatory investor meeting. With a sense of dread—the prescience he's talked about in a number of interviews—Jaako feels close to death and flies home, missing the required meeting by a couple hours. When he walks into the design studio, he's jumped and roughed up by this immense muscular brute in a robe. His muscles look like bells. The whole thing is bewildering.

Jaakko has Robin sketch the mystery woman who brought the meting summons. The two go on the offensive, breaking from their preparations for their follow up collection to head this thing off at the pass.

When Robin's woman again shows up again at the design studio, Jaakko and Robin hide themselves in a back room, peering at her verbal thrashing of their secretary through the window. Then, veiling themselves in samples from F/W '92, they head after her. Jaakko chose the delicate British rose print maxi dress and Robin selected the burnt umber jumpsuit with stovepipe legs. Both men wore their hair long. If the woman, whom we'll meet shortly, did catch a glimpse of the partners in her rearview mirror, of average height and sleight of build, with smudged-soft Raphaelian lips, it would have only provoked an insatiable covetousness for the foxy garments on the two fit models sashaying the blacktop.

The woman's name was Rowena Satie. A Columbia-educated financial analyst diversified into strongarm lackey, Satie was employed by The Guild, an investment firm with a wide-ranging portfolio of startups from BBQ restaurants in the southwest, to space exploration, to domestic leisure travel, to clothing, including a shelled and shielded trial investment in SPRAWLING ROBIN. More on that in a minute.

New to town from Vancouver, New Haven, Brussels—the rumors ranged—Rowena Satie proved an optimal enforcer for The Guild's predatory motions as she was unknown to most, easily underestimated with her mousse brown eyes under demuring bangs, comfortable with economic prevarication, and in possession of a finely-honed portfolio of judo throws.

The Guild was not exposed to the public until much later; until the organization's denuding in congressional grillings, which resulted in light community service for a number of top executives. But the odious profit-maximizing ambitions of the organization became actionable intelligence that very day for Jaakko and Robin as they followed Rowena Satie through the streets of downtown LA to The Guild's headquarters in nearby Downing; an infiltration unnoticed except by so many receptionists and executive assistants inquiring, "OMG that dress, who is that?" or "Vintage Balmain? shut up — no way it's new. By who?" to which the two models could only defer these harassments by citing their display of a forthcoming collection from a designer named "Disguise" which soon evolved to include the nobiliary particle, "De," as in "De Guise," while all the while trying to keep eyes on their mark, who was snaking her way through a top-of-the-hour throng of attorneys and prospective clients exiting conference rooms to a long hallway with mirrored floors; floors so clean they could veritably be labeled *lewd*. And at one of these doors, Satie paused and motioned familiarly towards a man approaching from the opposite end of the long hallway.

The man was Robin Schwartz's father. Far enough away, he's unable to recognize his son and his shoulder length blonde hair, now pulled into a totem pole top-bun, and neither was he able to identify Jaakko without his customary uniform suit, tight pants, the white boots. But greeting Rowena Satie with a kiss on the cheek, Robin's father motioned for her to enter the conference room, then rocked back on his heels long enough to admire her ass.

The deck had been stacked but the cards not yet dealt. Jaakko and Robin—in an orchestration of legal upper-handedness and with an admirable agility of mind—leveraged their current ownership stake while The Guild's coercion had not yet forced it from them and drove straight to the Board of Equalization office in Irvine, where they filed the dissolution paperwork of SPRAWLING ROBIN; a certainly antagonistic motion towards The Guild, but with such a courageous posture it required an exposure not clear its value to The Guild in counterpunch. Then, with that same BOE representative, Jaakko and Robin set to public record and taxman-oversight a limited liability corporation, self-capitalized by the virtually unknown riches of Jaakko himself, the genesis of which we know today as the inimitable House of De Guise...

Raheem paused, allowing for a long drink from his thermos. I had eaten nearly the entirety of his desktop bowl of pistachios, leaving a small mountain of shells on an unfolded cocktail napkin. I started in on the crystal goblet of wedding mints. While it seemed some pun, Klineman's inscription in my book morphed in implication. I was sweating, unable to stop. Raheem offered me a tissue, but I needed exercise. And a shave, a rinse, and some time facedown on the balcony.

∞ ∞ ∞

When I returned home, the treehouse was empty. Not a mew from Headlight, nor suggestion from The Old Man. Not a towel, not a bag of Celestial Seasonings in the kitchen drawer, not an artifact from antiquity cataloged on the living room shelves. Not the shelves themselves. Every last thing, save the phone plugged into the wall, was gone.

∞ ∞ ∞

IX

SUNLIGHT HIT THE FAN.

The phone rang. It's been ringing: suggestions, opportunities, casting agents, surveys, marketing scams, cult recruitment, leads, sightings.

I've compiled a new collection for the treehouse from around Beachwood. A labor of love:

a biodegradable coffee bag from Gelson's
paper towel cardboard rolls
a shredded sleeve of gabardine
chickpeas softened by what smells like Greek dressing
the crinkled foil of an un-crumpled gum wrapper
a broken glue gun
a tripod
sea shells in a plastic baggie
an unmarked VHS
ossified marshmallows
a broken croquet mallet
a box of toothpicks
a bag, mostly leaves, of yard debris
a crimson women's left pump
dual phonographs
a black flip phone
a shoebox of receipts

On one outing to gather supplies, I followed his tail like a swirling steadicam shot through the undergrowth, beneath rotted decks and behind groupings of hedges, up the sharp angling turns of the canyon roads and onto the upper parts of the mountain, past a soiree in the backyard of a small cottage and its drooping white lantern lights and the dozen bobbing heads of tipsy guests, then further upwards, passing within a few feet of a couple entwined on a beach blanket.

Then—the sounds by which I knew him best.

Grim mastications. A hiss. A gummy and excitable gibber. The muscular flexing of his grips. His padded roam lasted long enough for me to see him snake across a small crevasse, and in a clearing, raise his head. I tumbled, tearing my suit jacket, but came up on my feet as the possum, Ultimo, disappeared head-first into an open roadside trash bin, his grey hairless tail twirling above the rim.

Alongside the trash bin stood three green recycling cans. I left Ultimo to his dirty business and borrowed one to further my collection. Venturing with care down the steep and winding streets, I raided the other cans at curbside.

Back in my treehouse, I traded the lights for a low, bright moon. The can's oversized all-terrain wheels, caked with mud, streaked the hardwood. Once the cans were unpacked, I looked over the perilous descent off the balcony for some time. Then I disposed of the container into the abyss.

The phone rang.

Arranging this corpus around the room, I began my assemblage.

∞ ∞ ∞

X

SUNLIGHT HIT MY FACE. I answered the door.

Fauve.

Where are your clothes? Why haven't you answered my calls?

Fauve, in the flesh. We hadn't spoken since Bonnie Lu's with Klineman.

Somewhere, somewhere back there, I said, stepping outside and closing the door.

Don't be rude. Aren't you going to let me in?

The creations I'd made from the garbage—the sculptures as I'd left them—flashed through murky mind. Sorry, I said...probably best to stay out here. Rodent problem.

But Fauve was undaunted. You look like hell, she said. I do like the whiskers but what the hell did you do to your hair? Why don't we clean you up? Maybe go full-Willis and shave off the sides?

I ignored Fauve's dig. I am not one for mayhem.

Here, I have something for you, Fauve said. She reached inside a designer hobo bag for a large manila envelope. Her eyes were hidden behind sunglasses, but I imagined them like the two sides of an hourglass turned sideways, tipping time back and forth. You can play in the sand, I realized then and there, but that doesn't mean you get to go to the beach.

I'm not ready for anything new, I said.

But it's a request. You love requests. Remember what happened on the balcony the last time I gave you a request?

I'm booked...unless...is it about de Guy?

More important. Actually, I ought to give an update there, too.

I saw you in the *Times*, in the black dress. You looked beautiful. What was that designer's name?

I missed it. I do so many of these now, you know. Do you have a copy?

Not on me.

Do you want this envelope?

Not particularly.

Want me to leave it?

Sincerely, I'm busy. I'm working on something else.

Do you want to tell me about what you're working on? We could go look, then maybe brunch?

.

.

.

OK, give me the envelope.

∞ ∞ ∞

Fauve's envelope contained a roundtrip ticket to D.C. and a dossier concerning J.M. McGee, alias "Johnny Markers," alias "Buzzard," alias, "Babylon," who under investigation by the FCC, scrutiny by the FDA, audit by the IRS, and verdant criticism from the FRC, had vanished from his New Mexico compound. Last sighting: D.C.

With the treehouse desolate of my companions, I had no water or food bowls to fill, no one to counsel, no clothes to pack. And so I visited Raheem, and he fitted me in two loaner suits, filled my breast pocket with pistachios, and saw me to the airport where I boarded the plane on Fauve's, or someone's, dime.

∞ ∞ ∞

Fauve's honorarium was generous: First Class tickets, a meal of sous vide white fish with asparagus, cocktails gratis. I felt weighty in the seat, room to scoot.

The flight served Vernor's, a ginger ale best with bourbon, and by the time I exited, it was with a swerve in my step. The cab driver knew of a hotel, but I asked to be driven to a bar of his choosing for a nightcap. We arrived as the aftershocks of a day in politics spilled in; ties undone, the bootlickers vied for the lone bartender's attention with sort of juiced-up running back maneuvers.

There was some celebrity treatment of me here, the close shave a consistent baseline amongst this crowd, producing barrages of complements, uncomfortably envious stares, and gallant hands extended to prove the authenticity of my thick bristles over some work-stress hallucination.

Meanwhile, a woman lushly-fringed stared on. Whiskey gingers were ordered for me with Vernor's, complement of choice, as it goes, in the dens of lions. She winked. I winked back, slow and haphazard, like the uneven drawing of two begrimed shades.

∞ ∞ ∞

The cabbie woke me when we reached the hotel. I was greeted by name by the concierge though I had no reservation.

∞ ∞ ∞

The fringed woman from the bar, she wore a trench coat, and she had a lot of nice things to say, which was great. She said yes to a mini-bar gin, though I'd imagined her a pinot noir lady. Before she arrived in her cab, I phoned the front desk for advice on a movie; told the concierge I'd be entertaining. We browsed the night's cable listings over the phone, and from the available classics, he assured we wouldn't miss with *Weekend at Bernie's*.

Lacking any knowledge of pace and custom when entertaining a recently acquainted woman, I thought to lead strong and left my checkbook open to its reconciliation page atop the bathroom sink. We sat under a blanket together and ate late night pizza. I had a lot of clever comments to make about the movie, and she was quick with incisive responses, which was great.

We paused the movie a couple times so I could relieve myself. I noticed she hadn't looked through the checkbook yet, and I moved it to the top of the toilet where she'd see it with certainty. When I returned, she'd peeled the label from her beer, leaving the green bottle sad on the suite's coffee table. I couldn't stand the sight and put the bottle back in the mini fridge.

She suggested we kiss. I told her I'd hoped we'd finish the movie, but yes. It's not that I found her unattractive, not at all, but that I could imagine a second night together, with less pizza and Vernor's, after I knew she'd seen my checkbook. When we embraced and her arms wrapped around my body, she seemed inspired by the film and heaved me from the couch in a judo-like toss. I landed on my back on the table but maintaining a hold on her arm, lunged forward and found her neck with my red mouth. She flipped me again, pretzeling my arm. Was this pain or pleasure? When I thought of Fauve, I turned aside and spat.

∞ ∞ ∞

The phone rang.

Fauve, angry Fauve.

What the fuck are these things? she said.

My head, an agony. I fell back to the sheets. The receiver smelled like Listerine. Raheem's second suit hung on the hotel's bathroom door, and I still wore the first. The room was demolished, as though visited by one of those tornadoes of Jaakko's, and all I could remember is that somehow a kiss and a film had turned into very unsexy combat. My eyes settled on a familiar name emblazoned in goldleaf on the front of a navy calling card left on the nightstand. Rowena Satie.

Fauve again, through the receiver. I'm calling from your living room. Can you explain to me what I'm looking at?

I'd be interested in your impressions.

Um, well, it's me. You've built you and me. From garbage.

Some garbage, but also other things.

These are like life-sized dolls. Is this some kind of present for me?

Not really.

Or like an art project?

Why are you in my house?

I came over to check on Headlight. You seemed a little unhinged when I gave you the request.

Maybe you've missed the posters on every corner in Beachwood. Headlight is gone.

Gone how? Headlight is in my lap.

I sat bolt upright in bed.

Now tell me, Fauve said, what are these trash people all about? And where is your furniture?

∞ ∞ ∞

I boarded the first flight back to LAX, caught a cab to Beachwood. When I opened the door, the treehouse was as I'd left it. In the middle of the living room stood the assemblages of Fauve and me: a black trash bag for her mini dress, the monochrome daisy from the night the Klineman Affair began repainted in White Out, a tripod expanded for her legs, a taxidermied boar head with broken tusks for her head, her hair affixed to its sides from landscaped pussywillows.

In the corner of the room was a sleeping bag. Fauve must have spent the night. And in a lump at the bottom of the bag, zipped and warm, slept my beloved Headlight.

∞ ∞ ∞

It was the strangest thing.

Fauve on the phone. Headlight on the windowsill. Reunited, we were working on the Missing/Reward posters for The Old Man when Fauve called.

When you were in D.C. and I slept in the living room with Headlight, there was a moon so bright I could see without the lights on. Which was useful since you don't have any lightbulbs. Nor lamps now that I think about it. Your sculptures were standing there, and I was looking at them, and I was trying to fall asleep, and I started playing this game to help me. I call it...don't laugh.

I won't.

I call it ZOOM. It's hard to explain, but I imagine myself as being like a camera, and the game starts with me-as-camera on top of a marble; a black shooter marble. And I'm shot at a group of other marbles, then when I hit the group, I follow one of the offshoots, which will then roll off of a table and zip down onto a rollercoaster track and fire into the sky, and it will hit a plane, which then plummets to the earth, but the passengers jump out and pull parachutes, and I ride in one of their vantage points, but the parachute rips, and I plummet but land in the mouth of a pelican, which swan dives and spits me into the cab of a convertible, which then jumps the Grand Canyon. It just goes like this and it's different every time. I try to just let my mind let go.

Sounds stressful for sleeping.

It sounds that way, but when I'm not trying to control it, it's not... but anyways, what happened is this. I started playing ZOOM in your living room that night. I'm the shooter marble, and I strike the group, but instead of rolling off the table to start the game, my perspective shoots up this mechanical tower. It's grey and separated into three legs. I go up one, down the other towards the ground, then back up the third into a black abyss, illuminated with little pockets of light, and I can make out fields of flowers inside. There's a hole, and I burst out of it and behind me there's a herd of swine, and I never encounter other creatures in ZOOM, and I am terrified. They are full of holes, massacred, blood is everywhere, and my marble is frozen while they charge closer. I'm standing in a field of wheat, and I can see the ground behind them. It's ravaged, churned-up, blighted, and I know that when they hit me, I will die.

What happened?

I felt this grinding on my hands, then a quick prick like an acupuncture needle, but as though the practitioner was dragging the needle once inside, widening the hole. I looked down at my hand, and it was Headlight, her claws in my palm, licking between my fingers with her sandpaper tongue.

I got up and went to the bathroom. I was soaked through with sweat, and by the way, you don't have toilet paper or towels or toothpaste or anything, and I looked at myself in the mirror, and all I could see were these giant teeth. They seemed to take up my whole face. My arms looked like spindly bones. And my hair was thin, and dry, and brittle.

I left. Drove around all night, and ended up in Ojai. I was frightened out of my mind. I called Klineman, and then went by his house, but the RV was gone, and he didn't pick up. I ended up lying on a blanket at the beach, and I didn't fall asleep until the sun was rising.

∞ ∞ ∞

XI

A TIP COMES IN REGARDING THE OLD MAN. It's from Klineman. He is delivering a keynote at UMASS—though a quick check afterwards of one of his usual haunts confirms he's on the troubadour's circuit—and on a day of leisure, he decides to visit a string of antique stores on Pleasant St. There, he checks out a boutique specializing in rarities, and while he's browsing, sights The Old Man on a shelf behind the counter, flanked on either side by funeral urns. Klineman must have betrayed his interest as the proprietor was evasive on the price. But the good Doc pressed him and the shopkeep finally named some exorbitant figure.

I bought it back for you, Klineman said. Thought I might owe you one. When's a good time?

I looked around the treehouse, at the sculptures of Fauve of the Creature and me, and Headlight, now perched atop her boar's head.

Well, Doc, I'm free anytime.

I could use a drive. I'll come to you. Let's make lunch.

∞ ∞ ∞

The matter of de Guy / De Guise persists. Now, the short-shifted McGee BBQ Investigation, complicated by a trained assassin who doesn't appreciate a careful ledger, along with this Round Two of The Klineman Affair. Fauve's dossiers are slim. Jillian Carbess isn't answering.

Klineman and I have agreed to meet at Beachwood Market. I've just parked when chugging next to me in the RV, wearing a palm tree shirt and plastic hot pink sunglasses, a hairy arm hanging out the window, is the eager Professor.

Hungry?

∞ ∞ ∞

The RV had been professionally cleaned since my last visit. Klineman gestures toward the swiveling third chair of the vessel just to the inside-right of the door; the chair in which I tonsured the undergraduate's hair. He holds out two uncapped Bartles and Jaymes: a Mai Tai and a Sex on the Beach, and gestures toward a particle-board side table.

I believe this belongs to you.

The Old Man. He looks a little battered, bewildered too, but intact. Headlight leaps from my arms, lands on the ground, and springs on top of our old friend.

This is very kind.

Don't mention it. We should speak alone sometimes, just you and I, without Fauve. I thought you may get in touch sooner but you never showed. Get my message? The one in the book?

De Guise?

Tacky, I know. Of course, I'm fond of Jaako but naming an empire off wordplay is a bit much. But our side wouldn't survive without him. I had to speak indirectly, too, since I am surveilled in perpetuity.

Your fan club.

They do appreciable work. A kept professor could fare much worse in assigned assistants. The top brass in *De Rerum Canetis* keep close tabs on all our people these days. Not sure who they can trust, what with so many people going missing and so many more looking for them, and then they disappear, and the cycle goes on ad infinitum until both our sides are out of agents, not from warfare but on account of getting lost, or distracted, or forgetting which side they were on in the first place. We've been at it for centuries, and finally Jaako is putting a stake in the ground. Enough is enough. Time to find McGee. Draw this thing to a close. So I'm not complaining if the boys upstairs want to make sure I stick around. Mayonnaise?

No thanks. Fauve had me looking for McGee. I just returned.

His back to me, Klineman stops slicing. His voice is drawn, short of breath, but full of wonder.

Did she now? I wonder on who's authority?

The moment passed, and he regained his composure and all his jolly charm.

I've followed your work, you know. Fauve has told me stories. I'm an admirer.

We share that then.

When he spins back around, Klineman sets a Dagwood on the TV tray in front me. The precision of the sandwich is advertisement-worthy with its finely layered strata of turkey and roast beef, evenly sliced red onion, crisp butterleaf lettuce, two inclusions of cheese, thick slices of tomato, and slicks of Dijon mustard, held together by sourdough and toothpicks. Despite the architecture, the sandwich is tasteless.

We'll get to The Guild and McGee, Klineman says. I heard about your brush-up with Rowena Satie. That one will win you some points with Jaako. Consider this conversation an invitation to join a special kind of family. First thing though.

Klineman bites a monstrous chunk of his mirrored sandwich and talks through a full mouth.

I want to get your take on the madrigals.

∞ ∞ ∞

I didn't open up The Old Man until I got home. A makeshift funeral urn, he was filled to the brim with ashes that smelled of brown sugar, vinegar, Worcesteshire sauce, onion. Despite my disgust, I thought immediately of smoked brisket. And then I vomited off the balcony.

∞ ∞ ∞

XII

IT TOOK ME TIL SATURDAY NOON TO LEAVE the treehouse for a salad niçoise at La Poubelle. Three days locked up, replenishing from a Harney & Sons sampler pack, a gift from Jillian, righted my thereins and put to order the machinations of clandestine factions and all the curving tunnels of their waterparks, their sky ambitions, their barbecue, and their women's clothing. Sometimes you're given a mark. But then in the swirl of pursuit, the table is reset, and when everyone shows up for your dinner party, you find you've been the guest of honor all along.

I wanted no part of it. I wanted a stainless steel straight razor, warm water, and a basin of shaving cream. I wanted the off-request from a concerned sister, and to exhibit my sculptures in San Francisco, and to sautée kale for Fauve.

Begin again, that's what Jillian would say. That, and start small. You're good at this. You can manage your thereins. Mann, you have a future.

From my driver's seat, I observed a Mercedes cave-in the left fender of a Corolla, rock forward into gear, pause, then speed from the lot. From a page in my steno pad, I left the plate number on the Corolla's windshield.

I then examined a satiated tick and removed it from behind Headlight's ear. She padded at the thing on the floorboards of the car, then plunged one sharp claw into its swollen body.

Children wearing faerie wings, faces smeared with ketchup, ate hamburgers on the outdoor tables at Ruby's Diner. One said, I will be the Bad Bug. The second cried, I am Seasalt, Queen of the Seahorses. The third said, call me Panda-Boy.

I took several pages of notes in a median under a group of shaved palm trees in Pasadena. Then, I located and returned to its owner a missing Cocker Spaniel named Empress.

Then, I took to the dreaded DMV to renew my registration.

The old man, I said to Headlight and to The Old Man, is back again.

SWERVE FOUR

...And so on.

I put the paperback down and took up my notebook. It occurred to me, however, that before I wrote anything down, I should read the book again. There was something vaguely familiar about the story, and I tend to believe, or must believe, that the traces of a path remain and walking it means that one need only to walk. I felt suddenly that the world of the book and the people in it made the same choices, and each walked a path and that the same one could be found just outside the garage window, down the road, past the small barbershop on the corner. Do characters make choices? Do they change faces; do they move through walls, so to speak? Can we do this, then? I looked at the triangles and the spiral and turned to a clean page in my notebook and tried to draw a simple line that followed each path I walked in each town, but this didn't help and was too complicated to remember accurately. I wrote everyone's name that I could remember down vertically, then tried to come up with words that began with each of the letters and then tried doing a word search in the resulting letters. The photograph fell out of the notebook, and I picked it up, looked at it again, and then caught sight of myself in the reflection of the safety window between the office and the garage. There was something about my face: there was ink all over it, and, I then noticed, all over my fingers. I looked at the pen and noticed that, while I was lost in thought, that I'd flipped a lever on the side of the pen up, which in turn, squirted ink all over my hands and spread along the paths of my hands as I pulled and probed my face in thought. I copied this path into my notebook, but the page was hopelessly smeared and dotted. Later, as I was trying to clean off my face with a napkin dipped in cold coffee, the mechanic came in and told me someone had put sugar in poor Torito's gas tank. Probably some hippy-dippy tree huggers, he said, we get a lot of them around here for some reason, live up in some house all together. One of them up and drowned in a river not long ago, trying to hang a banner for plant rights—they found her with pockets full of things like rosemary and thyme and other wacko drugs. The disgusting man laughed, brown spittle raining in a mentholated haze, while handing me the substantial bill.

Torito had a strange smell now, and I had to drive with the windows down. After being on the highway for several hours—with Torito snorting and snarling at the rear bumpers of nearby cars and occasionally drifting into the shoulder in a hypoglycemic torpor—I figured that I should pull over at a rest stop with lots of shade and give the little muscle car a rest under a tree. As I was getting out, I noticed the mechanic's spit cup had spilled all over the passenger side floorboard and cascaded and pooled beneath the seat. There were no paper towels in the rest stop bathroom, but I did find a dirty tee shirt in one of the trashcans that I rinsed in the small creek behind the gazebo as the sun was setting. I spent the next hour or so attempting to clean up the spill, until it was too dark to see, and, like so many times before, I curled up in the embrace of Torito's strong and comforting back seat.

IX

THERE WAS A PLEASANT AND SURPRISING ABUNDANCE of birdsong floating above the highway rest stop. I walked to the little stream that ran behind the block of toilets and a small gazebo nearby. It wasn't quite dawn, and I walked over there to wake up a little. On the way, I bought four iced coffee drinks, two bags of peanuts, and a bag of pretzels from the pair of bright vending machines. I sat there and listened to the wind, smelled the morning around me, the grass, and the slightly sweet smell of the creek. All the birds sang their songs of the dawn. I saw a family of rabbits in the field across the water. The coffee drink was too sweet but it did help in waking me up. I realized, before leaving the warm embrace of Torito, that I'd been so busy trying to clean my face, that I'd left the paperback of *Avalanche* at the mechanic's. When I was awake enough, I opened my notebook again and tried to restructure what I'd been mapping out, including which chapters of the book I could remember, which wasn't much. It was like it had been flushed from my brain in the night, and I regretted not taking notes. By now, I thought, there must be some relationship that I wasn't connecting. Then I drank a second coffee and ate the bag of pretzels, which deliciously soaked up the sweetness of the drink. The fountain pen was almost out of ink, and so I first rinsed the dried ink off the barrel and nib, then tentatively worked the lever, which moved a piston and compressed a chamber of some sort inside it, which must be how it was refilled. I flicked the lever up, held it under the bare dribble of water from the bathroom sink and slowly pressed the lever back into place, filling it up. I tried it out by sketching the creek. The ink came out a pale purple, but still more visible than I had imagined, and while I was trying to draw the ripples in the current of the creek, I remembered that I'd once seen somewhere in a book on something called systems thinking—a book I couldn't quite comprehend—that there was a way of mapping out ideas, events, influences, and so on, which was what I'd basically been doing, but with the addition of small symbols along each connection to show how one point affected the other. So I tried this on a new page, writing positive influences with a (+) and negative ones with the symbol (–). These positive and negative relationships were easy enough to note, but then I decided to go further and try to figure out which connections were true (=) and which were false (≠). After an hour or two of carefully weighing the evidence and connections thus far, I encountered and reviewed the map I'd made, feeling a sense of dogged analytical triumph only to find that I had marked every connection to be both true and false relative to the simultaneously positive and negative relationships. I tried making a series of columns, as one would for a mystery-themed board game or logic puzzle, with a large grid placing the same symbols for true, untrue, negative, and positive in the boxes, but in the end it showed only the most obvious relationships.

I was flipping back and forth through the pages of the notebook when someone said, What are you reading?

I looked up to find a woman with a large backpack standing at the edge of the gazebo. I must have been too absorbed to notice her.

It's just a notebook, I said, I was just collecting my thoughts.

I don't know that you're doing such a good job at it. It looks like a real mess.

I looked down. It works better in my other line of work, I said.

Oh, your day job as a rest stop attendant?

I think that's an almost perfect description, I said.

And this is your hobby? Collecting your thoughts by making diagrams and charts?

No, this is my other job.

Have you tried drawing a picture? she suggested.

No, does that work?

Works for me. But then again, that's the way I think. I think in pictures.

Are you an artist, then? What are you doing out here?

I'm getting my MFA in painting, but I feel I'm moving away from it a little. I was just on a research trip and found out more than I could have hoped for, but we ran out of money because I just kept wanting to find out more. So now we're hitching back to school, she said.

Hitchhiking? I never went hitchhiking.

You're not dead yet; there's still time to find yourself as a hitchhiker, she smiled her voice sounded familiar.

What were you researching?

I'm tracing a family tree in a way, she said.

You don't do telemarketing, do you?

No, work-study at my school. Listen, can you give us a lift? Me and Clive. We can't chip in for gas, but I can tell you about what I found out.

That sounds like a plan, I said.

Great, she said, and looked over my shoulder at something. I'm Maude.

Guy, I said.

Clive is over there, she pointed towards a picnic table near the parking lot.

We started walking towards Torito, who seemed content with the blue sky reflecting in the windshield. I pointed the car out and then went to buy two more iced coffee drinks. When I returned, there was a man standing with the woman. He was in tight jeans, a snorkel jacket, and a stocking cap despite the warm weather. This is Clive. He kind of held out his hand then let it drop again.

Sure, I said, Torito has plenty of room.

That's so sweet, she said, taking my two iced coffee drinks and handing one to Clive. I thought about going back to get more, but they already had the doors open, and I worried that I would maybe look like a creep now that I was thinking about it.

Shotgun, the Clive said, as if he was falling asleep already in the front seat.

Once we were going down the highway at a pretty good pace, I thought I'd get the conversation going. Clive, I said, What do you do?

He's a conceptual artist, Maude said.

Oh? What's conceptual art, I said.

Whatever, Clive said, I mean, it's stupid. It's just art. I don't even like to think about it.

He's brilliant, Maude said, All his work is just so duh. You're just there with it. I wish I could do something like that. I'm always just so up in my head when I'm trying to work.

Like this research you are doing, I said.

Yeah. We have to hitchhike because I'm in all in my head, she said, but at least it's been fun. We've been hitchhiking for—I don't even know. Can you roll down the window?

Sure, I said.

I rolled down the front windows about one-quarter way. Clive was on his phone.

Tell me about your research, I said.

My thesis, Maude said. I had no idea what I was going to do, so I went and talked to my advisor, and they asked me to try and go to a place that I don't want to go for my thesis project. So, I thought about going back home to this place called Longing Lake. And we used to go to a festival they have every year when the lake freezes. One night I saw the butcher from the grocery store and his wife skating on the lake until the early morning, like moths on a pane of glass. Since then, I've never gone back for some reason. I told my advisor that, and they said, You need to go there. So, I got Clive to go with me, and we hitchhiked.

Did you find out why you didn't go back?

I have no idea, she said, But I did find out why they hold the festival, and I want to go back again when it's winter. So, the festival itself is mostly like any kind of fair, but it's at Longing Lake, and edges of the lake were filled with fish-themed booths, your usual carnival games, but ice and snow themed. A Ferris wheel, which is crazy in that cold. And on the lake itself there are all these fishing huts filled with men and women who are all trying to fish out treasure from the lake. Because that's the main thing, the weird treasure hunt that happens. I thought it was stupid, because why do it in the winter? Why can't you just swim down and get the treasure, right? The story goes that a woman by the name of Hermes Venkos came to town long ago. No one knew where she came from, and not only was her name Hermes, but she was there to find silver, not gold. But as it goes, Hermes would load up her goat-cart with two or three weeks of supplies and go off somewhere and then return a month later with exquisitely shaped pearls of silver, something like ball shot that had been carved out from the inside to look like small flowers curled into themselves. It was commonly understood that this was because Hermes was just using a bullet caster to pour the refined silver into, which a lot of people did back then, since it was an easy way to get a mostly regular weight cast and counted. And to mark it as hers, she scored the inside of the die with what came out to look like the floral design. Soon, Hermes must have had a lot of silver hidden away and would spend only a little of the pearls in town. But each time Hermes was in town, she was beset by thieves, long-lost relatives, and hucksters allowing her to invest in their schemes. Somehow, Hermes was able to avoid being killed, swindled, and saddled. For a time, at least. A man who styled himself something like a preacher, but of no definite denomination, named Thom Valen, mostly a stranger in town himself, one day came up with the claim that Hermes had made a pact with the Devil. That all she was casting was lead, but when she opened the mold, the Devil had changed it into silver and that there was no mine at all.

What do you believe? I asked.

I think it doesn't matter, she said, It adds up and spends all the same. Anyway, when Valen started repeating the story every Sunday, sometimes as a side-note to scripture, other times as an out-and-out rant, he started to get the attention of the all of the disgruntled men in town: the refused investors; the disowned relatives; and the thieves who could never get the drop on Hermes. And after a while, they all had joined the pious and paranoid chorus led by Valen. Because, she said, which do you believe? That you suck at getting rich and mining and this strange woman from who knows where is better than you? Or that she's in league with the Devil and that's why? So, soon Valen had the largest congregation in town, all shouting that Hermes was cheating them. And soon, the inevitable happened: one day, after Valen had devoted his entire so-called sermon to Hermes, he led a greedy mob to snatch up Hermes as soon as someone saw her gnarled old hat. And once they got ahold of her, of course, Hermes gave up all the silver she had worked so hard for. It was all in sacks that were in big crates. Everyone was happy, pulling out bag after bag of silver pearls, and that might have been the end—everyone would have carried off what they saw was their share of the silver, if it hadn't been for Valen, who ordered everyone to gather the silver up and carry it to a small barge that was in a nearby lake.

Longing Lake?

Longing Lake. They took the silver and Hermes and did as Valen said. Once they piled all the silver into the center of the barge, he then told them to pile it over with wood, which they did, thinking it was probably wise to hide the silver. It was only after he ordered them to tie up Hermes and to put her on top of the wood, and set it all on fire, did his followers revolt. Not for the life of Hermes, but because they'd lose the silver! There was a sudden brawl on the shore. Everyone was fighting everyone, but, in that chaos, Valen managed to sneak away, and he set the barge on fire then dove in the water and tried to tow it single-handed, to the center of the lake. The barge burned down and sank, and Valen, exhausted by the swim and having only a flaming barge to rest on, drowned.

And Hermes died too, in all that?

No one really knows. Only Valen would have seen what happened to her, and no doubt he wanted her burned at the stake. A day later Valen's body washed on the shore and people came across burnt pieces of wood along the edges of the lake for years, but no one has mentioned finding Hermes's body. Who knows what happened to her.

Wow, I said, and so that's what your thesis project is about?

No way, it's only why they have the Longing Lake winter festival. Clive chortled.

My project emerged from a question: where did the silver come from? If it was real, I mean. The thing I found most beautiful were the descriptions of the silver pearls. I don't think they were cast from a ball-shot die. I think they really were flowers—or leaves that had dried and curled up into small pearls. Have you ever had real gunpowder green tea? There is a place by school that has it, and before you pour water over them, they look like ball shot, and then when you pour water over them, they bloom into tea leaves. So, I thought, maybe it wasn't a silver mine at all, but a silver forest that Hermes got her treasure from. And once I thought about this, I remembered a story I'd heard from my uncle, who is interested in these things. He spends half his life watching those reality shows about treasure hunting.

Ok, so let me try and trace this for you. The story goes like this: back in the early 17th century, an expedition returned to Spain carrying chests of silver. The expedition had been led by Diego Nuñez de Belalcázar. So according to the show my uncle watched, de Belalcázar was on a mission to find a lost group of missionaries led by Father Felix Enrique Vasquez, who had disappeared a decade before. Father Vasquez was said to have landed on an island somewhere broadly between Spain and present-day Florida. But, as soon as de Belalcázar arrived on this island, he began to hear stories about a city, not unlike the ones he had just left, built of stone and glass, silver and gold, located in a forest where even the sky was said to shimmer. Based on these rumors, he managed to compose rough sketches of what he was looking for: a city with large streets, towers, livestock, and what looked to be shepherds and supplicants. There was, he was surprised to discover, even what looked like Christian churches. Overwhelmed with the prospect of discovering a lost city founded, as de Belalcázar came to believe, by a lost group of Greek explorers, and, thinking that if he were still alive, that Father Vasquez would have no doubt taken refuge there, he set out towards the interior of the island.

They traveled the deceptively large island for half a year, and each person they encountered they asked about this great city, showing the pictures, and were told the same story: that somehow the city itself, it seemed, had traveled deeper in the island. Deciding that this was more a consequence of mistranslation than it was possible for a city to constantly move, the pace was slow and nearly half of the original expedition of 47 fell victim to broken limbs, disease, or were found mysteriously dead, killed by their own weapons.

Still, de Belalcázar was optimistic, encountering several positive portends, not least of which was a storm, where, as he stood in a clearing, it seemed the sky flashed silver. Two days later, he found a forest, whose leaves, it seemed, were made of silver.

In a small memoir, which I found, about his later life as a rabbit farmer, he wrote in a digression in the middle of a long revelry on how perfectly round rabbit poop is, that as a young man, standing in the forest, he'd had 'the sudden feeling that he was about to be pierced by thousands of delicate and shimmering spearheads.' But, after he held out his hand and let a leaf to land there, it wasn't silver, but a beautiful shade of shimmering pale green, and only when he rolled the leaf by the stem did it glimmer silver. He looked up, he wrote, as the wind blew through the trees and saw them shimmer. He and his men quickly chopped down as many trees as they could and bundled up the leaves in large chests before returning with their treasure, which was supposed to be a much-needed windfall, since the Eighty Years' War had nearly bankrupted Spain. Once home, after a harsh and long trip at sea de Belalcázar, soon found himself in a great drawing room standing amid large iron chests arranged in a crescent. After a short speech concerning their journey, the trunks were opened revealing not the great riches they had seen and collected in a frenzy but tied bundles of dried and brittle brown leaves—somehow the magic of the silver had vanished.

At first, the case was made that the sea journey had caused the silver to tarnish, like a crate of neglected spoons, but despite several attempts at burnishing the leaves to their former luster only to have them disintegrate and settle in the cracks of the stone floor and disappear beneath the heels of the court, the idea that the leaves were silver persisted. This belief allowed de Belalcázar to escape execution, to semi-retire as the head of the militia of a small town near the border, where soon he fell into raising rabbits. Meanwhile, interest in the leaves persisted. Some said that, if the leaves were bonded to wood with a resin sizing, they then could be polished without crumbling; others considered reducing the leaves by boiling them first in water or soaking them in alcohol before evaporating the liquid to retain the less soluble precious metal and thus reconstitute the precious remainder into bricks; still others attempted to use the same method of extracting silver from lead with similarly poor result. It was then that an alchemist named Cornelius Syvargentus was drafted into service to solve the problem. Although he was Dutch, he had long made his home in Spain and had won some fame after he had once won a wager with Emperor Rudolf II by making the summer air inside an abbey so cold that you could see your breath; there seemed to have been drifts of snowflakes. Reluctantly, I think, Syvargentus set out to solve the problem and came to believe the secret was not in what could be observed, but in what the observed indicated of what could not be observed, that the leaves themselves were not silver, but mere leaves, and instead that they possessed a quality of attracting the atomized silver that must be present only in the ether of the grove, giving them the appearance of solid silver. Syvargentus then performed a number of experiments with melting down silver coins in a crucible to create a vapor and then exposing the leaves to the fumes but could not get them to conduct the metal. He then tied two hollow reeds together in an L shape, one dipped in a solution of water, silver, and mercury, the other he put in his mouth. When he blew through one reed, the air, crossing the other reed, lifted the mercury and silver water and sprayed it in a mist over the leaves. Later, when he demonstrated this effect to the court, he felt that he had not only thoroughly solved the mystery, but had also spared his own life. Believing that his part in the silver forest mystery was over, he made plans to return to his laboratories and wait out the war. But this was not to be.

Syvargentus had so impressed the court that another expedition was ordered, this time with Syvergentus as part of the group, with the idea that if he were allowed to conduct experiments in the grove itself, this would be the only way to capture the silver in the atmosphere, since the leaves were worthless. And it was only Syvargentus, after all, who would have the skill to do this. The last reliable account of Syvargentus was by the captain of the ship that dropped him, a group of fifteen assistants, and a contingency of soldiers on the coast of the island. The captain watched the forlorn alchemist disappear into the forested edge of the island with the assistants carrying his large crates. He was never seen again and no one through the years had any word of his fate when another ship returned for his scheduled pick-up two years later. This was why, my uncle says, there is treasure on the island and why he wants to go and dig up every inch of it.

And you are going with him to do this? Can you do that for a thesis?

Nope, she said. There is another part of the story. Because, the silver forest might mean that Hermes found a shipwreck or something that had the treasure and that was where she was getting her silver pearls from, because they were actually leaves, and why they burned up in the fire at Longing Lake and anyone who fishes for silver there is foolish. My project has to do with what de Belalcázar's original mission was, before he found the silver forest.

This is getting complicated, I said, opening a coffee drink.

Thank you, Clive said.

Ok, so, why was de Belalcázar out there in the first place? To find the priest and his missionaries. So, who was he, I wondered, and went to look him up. The only thing I could find on Father Felix Enrique Vasquez was that, like so many of his time, little is known about him, except that he had studied art in Italy in the 16th century, under the apprenticeship of a painter who called himself Antonius who was, unfortunately, a strong critic of the Medici. After returning from Italy, he spent the next decade or more working on an illuminated Bible that, by many accounts, was said to have been the height of a man and three times his width when closed. He had a group of five novices whose sole jobs were to transport the book and to serve as lectern, with two kneeling and two standing with the book resting on their backs, and the fifth had the job to turn the pages whenever Father Vasquez was using it in any liturgical capacity. The scale alone was wonderous, but once opened, the book revealed itself to be full of such detailed imagery, and the pages so laden with gold and silver that each one seemed to be almost three dimensional. While contemplating a scene, the light would play upon the page giving life to the large streets, towers, castles, livestock, shepherds, and supplicants. The tome, given its size, must have weighed a ton, she said. Can you imagine it? Soon Father Vasquez felt that the book was being wasted on the Spanish cathedrals. He would travel from village to village with his book, then, once they arrived, Father Vasquez and his assistants would take a moment to rest, then clean and change into their vestments. And if it was still daylight, or the next morning, they would open the book, and as the sun dappled pages came to life, tell, in Latin, the stories of the life and death of the Savior, the great city of Jerusalem, the wars, punishments, and miracles, that the new converts would request to gaze upon the holy book again and again, and would often, it is said, grow concerned for the people and places they saw the previous day, only to be surprised at their resurrection a few pages back, or death a few pages forward, all in gory and minute detail. The illuminated pages, splendid in candlelight of cathedrals, was glorious in the shifting moods of the sun. Soon, the church decided that the spectacle of Father Vasquez's book would be put to use in the colonies across the ocean. Then, he and the book disappeared, and you know what happens next.

I thought the book idea was cool, and I decided that my thesis is going to be on this giant illuminated book.

But that was stupid, Clive said.

Yeah, it wasn't duh enough, Maude said, so Clive and I were at the mall, and I thought, here it is! My thesis project is going to be a series of illuminated pages of my family, but like they were photographed in the old photo studios they had in malls in the 80s? Like all those cheesy pictures you see that are all soft focused and sometimes have dogs and mullets in them? Like that, but gold-leafed and really big—as big as I can make them.

Wow, I said, feeling a little regret over drinking so many coffee drinks.

W-ow, Clive said. And the wow thing is that it's all fake, made up by the show to make it seem like there was some reason to dig up that whole island and have a show in the first place.

Yeah, Maude said, It was all for the show, and my uncle is stupid because he thinks it's true because it's on the show. But it doesn't matter.

It sounds interesting, I said, I hope I get to see it sometime.

There was a stretch of delinquent roadwork, and Torito's low slung carriage shook and rattled us with each rough spot. And with each bump and jostle my regret over the coffee drinks grew. We'd been on the road for about two hours, so I thought it was time for break anyway. Mind if I pull over a sec, I said and eased Torito into the grass just past the shoulder to graze a little.

Can you leave the stereo on? Clive said.

Sure thing, I said, and slipped the keys back in the ignition.

There wasn't a tree except for a cluster about a hundred yards away. If I didn't have passengers, I might have just used Torito's flank to hide the deed, but since they were right there, I decided it was best to hike a little to the trees. The walk was more than I had expected, and when I got to the trees, I looked up at the spreading boughs from where I stood at the trunk and even without them having silver leaves, they were magnificent. I think they were willows, twisting above me, as if they had joined in my momentary dancing.

When I got back to where I'd left Torito to graze, the little muscle car was no longer there, and neither were his wards. I didn't feel anger but surprise. Still, they had been polite enough to leave a coffee drink and my pen and notebook, which I found in the grass with a rock holding open a page that read: *Sorry, we had to follow the path given us, XO Maude and Clive.* Below it was a little sketch of me standing among the trees, and I had a sudden rush of two minds in that moment, the observer and the observed—myself looking at myself in the picture—and I wanted to make a note of it, but somehow I couldn't quite diagram the sensation. I tried first by drawing a series of parallel lines, then intersecting lines, then boxes, but when I drew lines connecting two of those boxes, it made a cube, which continuously flipped inside and out and then for a split second, was both inside and out at the same time. I felt my head rush again and closed the book.

I stuck out my thumb and walked along the gravel shoulder for a while, then stopped and drank the coffee drink and turned to a new page and drew a triangle again, then the inverted triangle as before, but this time, I drew the same figure across so that the apexes of each triangle met in the center and then the spiral again from the center and likely because I was starting to suffer from dehydration and a sugar crash, I drew a stem on the resulting figure and some leaves along the stem and then scolded myself for wasting a page in my notebook so full of wasted pages. I took my windbreaker off and folded it into a kind of shoulder bag and stuck out my thumb again.

X

IT'S A MATTER OF SCIENCE, the man in the coveralls was saying. I'd been trying unsuccessfully to hitchhike when, finally I resigned to come to my end and become a pile of bones on the side of the road, an RV pulled over, and out he stepped: Ros, offering me a ride. I was pleased to see that he'd gotten back his RV and, I soon discovered, his cats. The inside was more like a small house than I'd seen inside RVs. The walls were lined with books, and there was a brocade couch, whereupon was sleeping a knot of three or four cats, and a nice end table across from a small sink with fancy fixtures. The hanging baskets swayed, and it had the smell not of the inside of a car, but an apothecary from the herbs drying over the window. I couldn't see any further because a tapestry curtain seemed to divide what I imagined to be the bedroom from the main area, while allowing the cats to move freely between domains. By then we were heading down the highway at a pretty good clip for an RV, and I didn't really want to walk around too much inside. I'd already showed him the picture, told him about the job I was sort-of on, what happened to the car.

It's a matter of science, Ros continued, Have you ever heard of quantum being theory?

Quantum being? No, I said.

Well, you know, it's a revolutionary idea that isn't very popular because it's, well, it's hard to accept—it radically changes our every idea of reality. Ok, I think I'm freaking you out.

No, I said, I'm just a little skeptical.

Yes, he said, yes. As you should be, as one should be...But what I'm talking about here—ok, let me see if I can't construct this for you: So, one of the greatest challenges to quantum computing is that the smaller you get, the less predictable things get. So, if you try to build a circuit less than, say, five atoms, you can't be certain that the electron, which you need to get the circuit going, will be inside the circuit and not outside of it somewhere. Six atoms and boom, you got a regular and predictable movement of electrons; at something like five, and you got nothing—in fact, it seems that the electron is both inside the circuit and outside the circuit at the same time. Now this is the uncertainty principle—you just have to deal with it. Ever hear of Schrödinger's cat?

The cat, the box, the poison?

Yes, but I hate that it's a cat. So I like to think about it as Schrödinger's Fat Cat. So the Fat Cat is alive and dead at the same time, until you open the box and look, just like the electron. Or, you flip a coin, and, what is it? Heads or tails? It's a paradox so it's stupid. Until the idea finds its way, that it's not the observer that matters, but the observer is an observer in one world, while there is another observer in another world, each with their own memories and histories where each outcome is true.

I took out a coin and flipped it. Heads, I said.

Yes, and flip it again, what do you think?

Heads.

Right? So same thing, it's both heads and tails before you look, then you look and it's one or the other—now this seems just a novelty. But, he said. The RV swerved a little, and I got nervous for a second, as did a cat that seemed to have found itself beneath my dangling hand and who, it turned out I had been petting, at least since the last coin toss, but it seemed like I'd been doing it longer—when I stopped, I felt the absence of the fur.

That's Cowtail, by the way.

Hello, Cowtail, I said to the cat and picked her up. The little grey cat looked up, blinked and purred, then dug her claws into my leg.

So, he continued, so now what if you concentrated really hard and said to yourself, the coin will always be heads or the coin will always be tails?

It wouldn't matter—it might appear that it matters, but it's always fifty-fifty, I said.

Sure, or not—what if it is because you know that it will be fifty-fifty and as it gets to be heads a number of times, you get nervous and think, ok, it has to be tails soon and sure enough it's tails. And on the one hand, what does it matter there is another world with another observer, with another memory and so forth. Do you gamble?

No, I said.

Okay then, ever fly a jet? he said.

No.

Too bad—I had this idea of buying a plane, something like a decommissioned military cargo plane, something with in-flight fueling capability, which would be easy, and just stay up there—off the grid. But an RV isn't bad—it's the transposition of VR, right? Yeah, the RV makes sense in this VR world, but a plane would be nice, too. Although it would be a tradeoff: I don't think the cats would like the plane, but, on the other hand, we would age less in one according to the laws of time dilation...

What?

It's a consequence of relativity—they tested it with quantum clocks—but listen. Where was I?

Do I fly?

Yes, well—the Pentagon. So, you know those maverick pilots who can just do crazy things? You've heard about it—pilots who could not possibly pull out of something, and yet, there they are safe and sound, or helicopter pilots in Vietnam—it defied technical ability, it out stripped aerodynamics, and the generals, always intent on making a better killing machine, wanted to know what it was that made one pilot great and another serviceable, so to speak. What do you think it is?

What? Fluke? Improbability playing out? Air currents?

The pilot.

Well, yeah. The pilot.

No no, I mean it was the pilots. It was the pilots and their total belief in their own ability. Haven't you ever heard of Patton walking out in a hail of bullets and not getting even a nick? Or when Sitting Bull sat down in the middle of a battle and smoked a pipe, and then just strolled away? I mean I hate to use examples from war, but that's history for you...anyway the brass over at the Pentagon, rationalists all, had to say it was the pilot. So they teamed up with MIT, I think, to test this—it's too expensive to just have pilots go up, go into a spin or something and then either crash or not, so they had these pilots participate in whatever experiment MIT could come up with. Now this was classified for a long time. So what they did was set up a board with pins on it. And up top, colored balls were dropped, and at the bottom, there were these tubes that would collect the balls, which were also colored. Now, when you drop the ball, it bounces from pin to pin, so that it's going to just be haywire. And math predicted so many balls would fall here and there, you know. Well, these pilots and a control group were told to spend like two hours just watching these balls being dropped, but to concentrate and try to follow the balls tumbling and picture them tumbling into their correct coordinating colored slot. Sure enough, the pilots had a statistically improbable effect on the balls while the control group followed the predicted outcomes. This was mind blowing to the generals and the scientists at MIT, but was until recently, relegated to the realm of ESP studies, and so forth. Telekinesis. But, this is the thing: there is physics and there is ESP studies and they were oceans apart. One seen as a joke, the other scientific truth.

Shouldn't it be, scientific truth and joke?

He smiled at me. Look, he said, I have a book. And he unhooked a leather lanyard from the ceiling and lashed it to the steering wheel, got up and started to rummage in the cabinets. I put my hand on the wheel. The cat seemed put out and jumped from my lap.

Do you do this often, I said, do you just lash the wheel?

Yeah, how else are we supposed to take a crap or something?

Aren't you worried?

The cats would let one of us know. He returned and tossed a staple-bound book in my lap that looked to have been composed on a typewriter, interleaved with photocopied reports with the words classified stamped on it, that otherwise looked like standard science papers. There was no author.

He unhooked the leather strap and settled back in the seat. Another cat seemed to want my attention now. Oh man, he said, turning up the radio, you like Sylvia Platte? This song, 'I Wanna

Just Come Home With You,' is so good—it expresses the Freudian impulses in romantic pop songs by recognizing and inverting the objective infantilizing positions of the subject and object of desire. He tapped the wheel and sang along to the abhorrently auto-tuned a cappella while I looked through the book. There were a few words that stood out, but by and large it seemed to be a garbled collage of technical language.

Now remember the uncertainty thing? Ros continued, You have a coin? Now flip the coin, think heads. I mean, just believe it will be heads.

I flipped again. Heads, I said.

Ok, now just keep flipping, he said, just whenever you think to, flip the coin. Ok, now, quantum being is like a marriage between the two: that the coin will always be heads if you just assume the coin will always be heads. The electron will be there. The cat will always be alive. And this world will always be this world; because we assume the world is like this, we believe the world is like this, and here we are, all authors of this story, moving it forward with occasionally a swerve. He tugged the wheel, and Cowtail who had returned to my lap, anchored herself with her claws. I tried assuming I would get out of this RV alive.

So, what I'm saying—you believe this thing, this guy you are looking for, right? You think you'll find him?

I'm not really supposed to find him.

But you want to?

Only out of guilt, maybe. This is my first expense account, and it kind of feels like I'm spending a reward before doing anything. Maybe that's crazy.

The world is crazy because we all know the world is crazy, he said. So the world is crazy. Everything, everything you see here was first in someone's mind. I don't mean, like some kind of thing—I'm not even talking quantum being now—I mean, literally, everything was in someone's mind and then made, and it was so long ago we just accept that these are things that make sense—yet we still worry about people spitting in our food. Well, if we can't trust some teenager in a drive-thru, how can we even accept the drive-thru? It came from someone's mind. You see what I'm saying? Because it is here, because it is made, and we accept it because we know it as real from childhood; it doesn't mean it was a good idea, or that it wasn't just as much an idea as, I don't know, tasting your own ear-wax.

A pair of cats came rushing forward to join the one already in my lap.

Hey, Croll. Hey, Maillion. You have a nice nap? Ros asked the yawning cats.

Then I heard a rustling behind me and saw the tapestry curtain slide open. Good morning, a woman said. She was dressed likewise in blue coveralls with the name Ros stitched on her pocket. Who's this? she said.

Oh, this is just some Guy.

Guy, I said waving slightly. The cat bit my hand gently to remind me that I had other duties.

Guy, he said, this is Ros.

Nice to meet you, she said.

Ros? I thought you were Ros.

We're both Ros, he said. It seemed to make sense—they both had their hair cut the same, and, except for his mustache and boutonnière, they were about the same build.

We're both Ros, she said, yet, we are not both Ros. The Roses are for different things.

Such is life.

Such is life.

Such is life, I said.

What's Guy's story, Ros said, beyond being a cat-stand. I'm surprised Boots and Maddox aren't in on that love-fest. Which reminds me, have you seen Headlamp?

No, but you know how skittish he gets. It's funny because he's such a big cat.

Maine Coon, she said to me.

Maybe he's looking for a Mann, like Guy here.

Oh? Don't we know someone in New Mexico that's pretty cool?

No, he's in Silver Lake now—I think he bought that old storefront. But he's looking for Mann.

Too bad, Ros said, he's a good guy.

No, I tried to clarify, I'm on a job of sorts. I'm just looking for this man named Mann. I showed the new Ros the picture.

Oh, boy. Okay, I see, Ros said and exchanged a look with Ros.

Yup, and that's why I was telling Guy about QBT.

Well, this is a morning of surprises, she said, handing back the picture. Where are we?

Near St. Louis, I think, Ros said.

We should stop at The Derringer House. Doesn't it look a little like...

Ros, Ros said, thank you for being here with me.

No, no, Ros; thank you for being here with me.

Mind making a stop, Guy? It's this little bed and breakfast—but it's really nice there and Malachi saves all the cooking oil for us. Wish this rig were electric, but right now, it's all biodiesel.

I am in your hands, I said, because mine are full of cats.

XI

WE ARRIVED LATE, but I could see, even in the moonlight, the bed and breakfast was a large Deco mansion. It was an almost institutional four-story building with small slotted windows and a large double door entrance. The RV pulled into a service road that led to the back unlit lot. Ros and Ros parked around back. This is how we roll, Ros said.

When I got to the front entrance, I was met by Malachi, a tall, lanky, and distracted man, who led me to a central courtyard and up an interior staircase that led to my room, which for some reason was on the third floor, although it seemed to me that the establishment was vacant. Going up the stairs to my room, I asked him if there wasn't another room available. His strange reply was to ask then, What do you think this is, a hotel? I took this for whatever it was worth. At the top of the stairs, he suddenly turned and said, After all, you're lucky I was up. I just returned from where I was researching in a peculiar archive outside the Boston Commons, he said, which had in its archive a series of rare broadsides about Deguy, a pirate I've been working on a book about. At least two of those broadsides were believed to have been composed and printed by Benjamin Franklin during his early apprenticeship to his brother James, when he was 12 or an early 13 and was still enamored of such maritime adventures. Here we are, he said unlocking the door.

The room was as spacious as Ros had described, but it was considerably stuffy, so after nodding a thanks to Malachi, I opened as many of the windows as I could to air it out. Instead of staying there, I decided to go back downstairs and sit in the central courtyard to review my notes, although once I sat down, I found my pen was out of ink, which is all the same because so far I'd not really found much of Mann. Still, I felt close to something, wavering somewhere there on the edges of things. I looked at the drawing of myself under the trees. It really did have something, a kind of practiced detail or movement in the lines that made it feel like it could have been done by a Matisse or Lautrec. I thought then that I should try to draw the clues and see if that would help put things in perspective. I dug in the cushions and found an orange crayon and started on the first drawing. No sooner had the first few tentative lines been made, Malachi interrupted me, coming down the stairs with a couple of mugs of cocoa asking what I was doing.

Thought you'd like something to help you rest, he said. If you're anything like me, I'm sure you have a hard time winding down. My mind just keeps at it. For example, I'm really interested in this little bit of information I discovered just yesterday that Deguy, according to one broadside I looked at, had narrowly escaped capture in Boston Harbor by dressing as a woman and boarding a coach full of consumptives bound inland to Slide Mountain Sanatorium in the Catskills. It's no longer there, unfortunately. The broadside went on to trace Deguy's furtive retreat northwest though New York and into Canada or at the time, New France, which had a more lenient policy on pirates, well insofar as Deguy happened to favor engagement with fattened Spanish and English vessels over the leaner French ones and perhaps gambled on the possibility, with the right campaigning, he could be considered a privateer for the French Crown. Perfectly legal.

Is the name French, I said.

Deguy? Supposed to be Old Dutch, but it's also a kind of fake French. My theory is that it's a pseudonym—part of what I'm working on is to find out who Deguy really was and what happened to the Portuguese Galleon he captured. He laughed, Because, if an investigation doesn't end in gold, what's the point?

I leaned back in my seat and listened to Malachi's ramblings. The inside of the Deco fortress was quite beautiful. We were sitting in an interior central garden full of plants and flowers. All the flowers were closed up and asleep but for one vining plant with large white flowers. Above us there were two balconied levels: the top level where my room was located, and what looked like an additional floor whose windows were stained glass, and above that, an arcade of glass to allow light into the garden, but at night looks like jade.

Just then Malachi coughed and lit a cigarette. Cocoa ok? he asked. I nodded although I'd not yet taken a sip, then went back to my gazing at the windows above, but no sooner did he interrupt again.

I see you have a sketchbook there; are you an artist? Ros is always picking up artists. Just last month there was a nice couple here. So what's your story?

No, I said. I just thought I'd give drawing a try. I'm on a research trip too, in a manner.

Oh, what kind, he said.

I feel like I'm looking for a ghost, I said.

Ghost hunting, are you? I tried that a while back in my twenties. I got a few close calls, but nothing I could ever get on tape. I mean you get things on tape, but it's never what you want it to be. Clicks and static and something like voices now and then. Haven't encountered any here. But then again, I've kind of been desensitized. You have to be sensitive to find them.

I'm not looking for a ghost, per se; I'm more interested in shedding light on this eclipsed figure, I said. I am a kind of a detective. Here... I took the photo from my notebook and showed it to him.

Oh, I see. I see. I get the feeling you're about thirty-three, am I right? I had myself a moment when I was that age. But now I take care of this place. I get to travel when I want. I took up amateur archeology. I can show you all the stuff I've dug up around here, you wouldn't believe. He stubbed his cigarette out on his palm. It's always under your nose.

If you did find a ghost, what would you do with it?

People don't find ghosts, often.

Well, sure, but say you did? What would you do?

I'd say, now look here: where's the gold? He laughed again. Am I right? It's gold isn't it? Wouldn't you squirrel some gold around here? Look at this place. How about you?

I'm not sure what I'd ask.

Well, okay, he said, suit yourself. What would you ask yourself?

What can I ask myself that I don't already know the answer to?

Oh plenty, plenty, Malachi said. Just give it a try sometime.

I was relieved to see that he was done with his cocoa. His eyebrows raised, and I could see that a thought had just occurred to him, his lips parting as if he were practicing what he would say. An attic, he said.

An attic?

The superego of a house; yeah, it's a big one all right. Well, technically it's a fourth floor. It's where Ms. Derringer lived and worked and died. He drew out the last word.

I was curious about that. So it's not just stained glass?

Oh, no; those windows open, or used to. She had them sealed up after her death.

I looked up at them again and yawned. Bedtime, I said.

Yup, Malachi said, I'll walk you up.

We went up the steps, my back cramping, and when we reached the top landing and my room, I turned to say my goodnights.

Listen, it just occurred to me, walking up here, since you're a ghost hunter and all, maybe you'd like to see the attic before going to bed? It's kind of a museum, you could say; well, this whole place is kind of a museum, but everything on the fourth floor has been left there like it was when Ms. Kora Derringer passed. She had it sealed off when she died, the whole floor. A few years ago, I opened it up, out of curiosity—I couldn't help myself. Archaeology, you know. I don't show people the place, or even let on that I've opened the rooms, but since you know Ros, I figure you're good people. And if ever there was someone going to haunt a place, it would be Ms. Derringer, and it would be that fourth floor.

Although I was tired, I followed him as he went over and pulled down a narrow set of stairs from the ceiling and deftly climbed up them while he lit another cigarette. It was still dark, but he pushed a button on the wall, and the lights came to life and slowly the preserved attic dwelling of Kora Derringer, revealed itself. All around there were papers, pens, ink jars, prisms, charms, minerals, banners, small curio machines. I was momentarily startled by what turned out to not be a ghost, but a dress on a mannequin in the corner by a sealed window. After the initial shock, it seemed that this mannequin gave a sort of life to the otherwise dormant room.

You'll notice that the books are all on a number of philosophical and occult subjects, weapons, flora and fauna. She was quite a reader, he said, And a writer too. Right here, at this desk, in the span of only two years, she wrote all 36 volumes of her mystical novel, *The Glowing I, the Knowing Eye*. Malachi pointed to a set of books with transitioning burgundy to midnight blue leather binding set behind a large statue of an obscene Pierrot sporting a rather unsettling and comically large erection that was buttressed by a Y-shaped crutch. But, he said, with all this around, there was no more infamous a treasure than a small ticket stub Ms. Derringer kept in a small jade box tied with thin leather strips, Malachi informed me, that hasn't been opened for fear of the fragile binding disintegrating. He showed me the box resting, as it was in her lifetime, on her writing desk. The box Malachi held out to me was very common looking, carved in an unrefined and unfinished pedestrian sort of Art Nouveau style, the type I have seen in countless shops selling incense and yoga mats.

How do you know it's in there, I asked.

There is no doubt, Malachi said, it was the most important item of her collection. Why wouldn't it be there? He took a drag of his new cigarette and continued, in fact, one could say that it was her only possession, a collection of a single item. All the rest of what you see here is just the clutter that, like doves, has simply come to roost in the attic.

A ticket stub, I asked.

Yes, he said.

Then why not put it in something nicer, that gold box there on the desk for example? Why such a drab reliquary?

You really are no treasure hunter, are you? Look, you put the most worthless, least meaningful thing you have in the gold box because that's the first thing to go, but if it is something really important, something very valuable, you put it in something unremarkable, something like a crumpled shoebox or battered snuff tin or between the pages of a rotting book or in the toilet taped just under the lid of the water tank. Look here, he plucked the gold box from the desk and held it open for me. I couldn't tell exactly what it was inside, but there was a kind of unpleasant and paradoxical dry, wet smell coming from what looked to be some moldering ash of some sort. He snapped the lid shut and tossed it back on the desk. But this, he continued, what's in this box is the very ticket stub from the first time that Ms. Derringer encountered Madam Van Valsing, a mystic, recently come to America, having left the Far East under threat of the death penalty for discovering certain mystical laws, as she put it.

I had neither heard of the mystic nor of Derringer. The apartment was impressive, and while Malachi was busy with something, I surreptitiously refilled my pen from an old yet surprisingly still liquid jar of what turned out to be violet ink on her immaculate desk. There was a familiarity to it, and I almost sat down and started to write something, but caught myself. And then I thought of the Roses' RV, and all I could think of was the bedroom, which by now must have been well aired. I realized I must have been tired and standing somewhat catatonic until I felt warm breath on my neck and felt a gentle tug at my sleeve. I turned to see Malachi grinning, flapping a small leather journal at me. Look, here, he said, proof. You always need proof to support your claims. No better proof than Ms. Derringer's Diary, from 1926. He began to read:

Thursday, 20 May

Waiting for H. to come back from chess with Bertrand, it is already 7:45 and if it wasn't for these sorts of things generally starting late, we wouldn't have time to attend. As tends to happen, one's mind slips after a certain hour and becomes more susceptible to animal magnetism, or whatever they use at these things to trick you into believing some nonsense about ghosts and spirits. Still, it should be fun to be there with H. if she ever shows, she is so infatuated with Occultation especially if it involves mediums, and she is thrilled by mediums. What a settlement! Last evening was a characteristically jovial time and when poor Bertrand couldn't find his way out of the cluttered labyrinth of iron furniture so that he just sat there all day having to smoke pencil shavings, and if you were to believe him, even a few pages of his own book after running out of tobacco rather than push his way through the cast-iron brambles—I should have liked to have witnessed Viv's expression when she encountered him sitting there. I imagine it was completely normal. I think next year we should have even more interesting people visit the villa.

Malachi interrupted his reading, I'm sorry, I feel like I should've told you a few things about the place first. See, this was the 20s, you know; most people had gone over to Paris to enjoy the liquor and cheap rent, but Kora Derringer was in no need for cheap rent—this villa was built to her specifications, according to her vision. There was no great need for alcohol since Canada, as you know, is just up the way and plenty of whiskey with it, so she decided to stay and create a kind of, well, Parisian bohemia here. So, she would invite famous poets and writers, painters and sculptors, philosophers and historians to come stay here instead—forget the Algonquin, those were newspaper hacks; here, here was where art was made. Then Malachi started to laugh, and he casually let his cigarette drop to the floor where he squashed out the ember with his shoe. As he went to rub his hands together, it seemed that a new cigarette appeared between the same fingers, and I was amazed by how smooth the whole operation was as he raised it to his lips. I noticed, too, that it was somehow already lit. Sure, he continued, people thought it was just Ms. Derringer's way of competing in society with the Trasks. Still, it had more the air of experimentation. The courtyard, for a time, was full of tables and chairs as a kind of courtyard café, and there would be nude lectures from the balconies.

But anyway, he said, you asked why I said that about the ticket. And he read again from her diary:

Tuesday 25 May

To continue—I don't know why I should even really tell the story of what happened these last two, was it two? I check the date and I see that no, it was not two but five, nearly a whole week has passed since that night! This—this should be evidence enough for trepidation in laying down my observations of this string of evenings, and compulsion enough to deem it imperative that I do, if for anything my own sense of chronology as it feels to me as if I have been at sea, or asleep in the Catskills after a game of ninepin—H. showed up dreadfully late and we had just chanced upon a cab and took that rather than walking as we had planned since it was a beautiful spring evening, to make it to the event on time, but when we arrived it seemed as if the whole thing had been placed on hold, or like a nickelodeon, our arrival had somehow set it in motion and had we not come along everyone would have been there, like statues in a tomb.

Anyway, as soon as we arrived, the acquaintance of H.'s whom I never wanted to meet, met us at the door and it was then I realized how H. had found out about this new medium and I flushed with fury, but thought it uncouth, really, since I had arrived with H. and after having our coats, hats, and purses taken, we were thrust into a smaller room and H. and I ended up sitting together at the round table where we were seated, I didn't have much time to contemplate my course, because just as soon as we all were seated—and a reason I couldn't then make out who else was in attendance—the lights went out and candles burst to life on the table and there, suddenly, without a sound or even a sense that there was space enough, a beautiful woman who was made up younger than I suspected her age to be, and a queer gentleman who seemed to be of some Northern heritage if not a Dane, were suddenly sitting shoulder to shoulder with us all. I have to say, it was quite an exciting entrance, and after H., out of fright, clutched after me, thoughts of the acquaintance, though she was sitting just off to the right of us, left me or perhaps the feeling simply resituated itself. The mysterious woman was introduced as Madam Van Valsing, a name that did not fit the Egypto-Asiatic face lit by the flickering candles. The introductions were done by the gentlemen sitting beside her, a Viscount Felipe del Roy, who, I later found out at some point over these lost days, was simply referred to as the Viscount. By way of introducing the event, the Viscount gave an account of their meeting: They had traveled together since encountering each other in an opium den where there was said to have been a woman over 300 years old, but who was, by all appearances no more than 19. The Viscount was there to investigate his lineage thinking perhaps, since the woman had lived chiefly in Northern Africa, that she may have remembrances of his ancestors who had obtained his title in the late 15th Century helping to establish Spain out of the Mahometan ashes of Al-Andalus. Van Valsing, although a skeptic at the time, wanted to learn from her the secret of immortality, or debunk her as a charlatan. They lived with her for nearly 3 years, the Viscount furiously writing what became, The History of My Family as Dictated by an Eye Witness, and Van Valsing only studied the young woman until one night, Van Valsing discovered the secret of immortality. It was not merely a immortality of the flesh, although the woman herself is 300 years old, but that she belonged to a family dynasty whose inheritance of, not only a name and close resemblance, but also the memories of each generation with as much exactitude as possible so that by the time the women were 19, they had, in a way, lived the previous generations lives. After learning this, Madam saw the wisdom in it, and decided that it was no trick at all, the attractive young girl was indeed over 300 years old in the same way that nations grow old. For the next two decades they traveled the globe and Van Valsing it seemed had a preternatural inclination towards the absorption of the occult arts. They traveled back to Van Valsing's homeland, a small Baltic monarchy, just in time for the King and his family to be brutally murdered and the whole country consumed in a flaming revolution. Van Valsing, having blood ties to the monarchy, was exiled.

The rather too extended introduction ended with Madam Van Valsing rising and thanking us for our attendance and as she said this it seemed as if she were staring directly at me, through me, and being penetrated by those so familiar and foreign eyes, seemed to flush all the night's anxieties from my body in one great fountain that rushed out of the top of my head leaving me filled only with a new feeling, a strangely comforting one. My body felt light and I can barely remember what great mysteries were performed except that it seemed at times that Madam would speak in a lower masculine voice, her exotic lips moving out of syncopation with the words, as if she were speaking a strange language that was being translated in thin air—all the while the Viscount had taken out an oak board and began to carve along its surface with an engraved athame, working deeper into the wood impossibly delicate occult symbols. At some point H. and her acquaintance slipped out of the room, but surprisingly nothing in me stirred in the slightest so scintillating were the mysteries therein that I had not noticed...O what have I even begun!

I looked down at my watch and was surprised by how late it was— had we been in that little attic so long? I took my leave by offering a lame joke about wanting a refund if I do not use the room. Malachi didn't seem amused by it. His gentle and soft face seemed to have turned hard. His eyes, which previously had seemed a little distracted and curious, were now predatory points, and, in fact, I was a little overcome with the idea that he had taken a disproportionate offense at my lame joke and was readying to throw me down the steep and narrow attic steps before I had the chance to go down them at my own pace. I offered a simple addendum, Just joking. This place is incredible. I'd spend all day up here, but I'm falling asleep on my feet. Thank you for bringing me up here and reading the diary to me; it was such a great act of generosity. Kora seems like she was an interesting person.

Malachi's scowl turned to a smile, and he seemed again gentle. I see, he said, Did you really enjoy it? I haven't finished, you know, there is still quite a bit of the story left. Volumes and volumes left, he said laughing.

Maybe tomorrow. Depends on what the Roses are up to. You can finish the story, but I really need to get some sleep.

Of course. I forget sometimes not everyone has this gerbil-wheel brain of mine. Always spinning, you know. Would you like to take a book with you to read? he said putting his arm around my shoulder, if you're anything like me, you find you'll have a hard time sleeping. But, there are lots of books here, and you should feel free to take whatever you wish to your room with you.

You don't happen to have a book called *Avalanche*, do you?

Avalanche? Isn't that part of that cult out in Ojai? The Golden Dawn mixed with astral projection and alien architect theory?

I don't know, I said, I don't know any of that, really. It was recommended to me by a woman at a library book sale.

I don't doubt Ms. Derringer has a copy even if it was printed back then.

No, I think it's recent.

Oh, he said, Maybe you would like to take the diary with you to bed?

No, no, I couldn't. I can't see a time when I would even get to reading it.

No, take it with you. You can finish the story on your own. It's an interesting one. And let me tell you, the dreams you have after reading her writing. You're good people, after all, I can trust you with it, can't I? His eyes were sharp again. Just joking, he said finally. You can leave it in the room when you are done reading it.

I tried to laugh and said, Well in that case, how can I refuse?

I took the diary and went down the stairs to my now cold and drafty room. It was a strange feeling I had, a strange sense that I'd been there before—or maybe it was just a kind of confusion in my mind from reading the diary. Although I had expected to stay awake and read, I fell asleep before I could open the diary and drifted into strange dreams about coils of light and green water dancing around a midnight blue body.

XII

IN THE MORNING, I took a bath and put on the clean pair of coveralls. They fit well, and I noticed that they were softer than I imagined and had a subtle herringbone pattern. Now that I was cleaned up, I could tell how bad my Everyday Joe clothes smelled. I rolled them tightly and took the plastic liner out of the wastebasket by the desk, put the clothes in it, and, after pushing out the air, tied it off. By the time I went down to breakfast, Ros, Ros, and Malachi were already eating.

Well, looks like you drank the Kool-Aid, Malachi said, appraising my new outfit.

They fit, Ros said.

Nicely, I said sitting down.

Three of a kind, Malachi said serving me a breakfast of poached eggs topped with sauerkraut, beans and seared kale, fresh honeydew melon wedges, two cups of weak creamy tea, three undercooked sausages that were nevertheless very tasty, and finally almond stuffed dates with three demitasses of very strong black coffee. If anyone saw the three of you sitting here, dressed like that, they would think I'm having central heating installed.

No, we are the Three Musketeers, I said.

More like the Tres Pendejos, Ros said.

Speak for yourself, Ros, Ros said.

Malachi hopped up to refill my cup, load on more fruit, get more cream, between taking for himself sloppy mouthfuls of food. Oh, you know, that reminds me of something I read. I'm not sure if was related to Deguy, but when I was trying to track down that Portuguese Galleon, I found a little monograph, no more than maybe eighty pages, on famous missing ships that claimed to have found the wreck of the Portuguese Galleon won by Deguy. But I got to go back a little for this story to make sense, you see. Ever hear of a ship called *Três Pegas de Netuno?*

No, I said, but as soon as I said it, I reached for my notebook and flipped through my daily maps and found there the name, poorly rendered. It was too late to correct myself; however, the moment had passed, and Malachi torrentially continued:

According to this little book, the *Três Pegas de Netuno* was supposedly a Portuguese man-of-war, that was later captured by a privateer flying a Dutch flag, likely a false one. This sounds to me like it was the same ship that Deguy took, but that's where me and other folks differ. But in any event, it likely wasn't a difficult task to take over the ship—in a surviving diary, the *Três Pegas* was called the *Três Moleques* by its crew in reference to the apparent incompetence and arrogance of the captain and his two mates. I mean, old story, right, see Dürer or Plato. But by and large, it seemed to the author of the monograph, that whatever the men in charge said, the crew should do the opposite. And with each command came the desired result, reinforcing the arrogance and ignorance of the três moleques themselves. Anyway, the *Três Pegas,* (or *Moleques*) was on its return trip from what turned out to be a short-lived colony in South America when it disappeared or was attacked and captured by Deguy, depending on who you believe. Afterward the três moleques were placed in a lifeboat and set adrift while the gold and gun laden ship disappeared until three decades later. According to this little book, there was a story of a small sloop encountering the *Três Pegas,* and thinking the ship had been adrift and abandoned, three members of the small crew boarded what they believed to be a ghost ship. The men who boarded reported that although there was no trace of life on deck, as soon as they stepped foot onboard, they smelled an acrid scent, like sulfur and burning hair, but mixed, too, with the scent of rose and frankincense. The yards were intact, however, and while the wheel had been lashed with a thick leather strap that had hardened in the salt air, the compass glass had been smashed. The hatches were still sealed, and they found the guns were still intact, the cannon balls still stacked in ready, but except for a little corrosion, these armaments looked ready to fire. The only thing they found out of place was that the door leading to the officer's cabins was chained shut, and although this detail did nothing to dissuade the baleful atmosphere on deck, it did impede any search for the log book, or, as each man secretly hoped, riches below. The men then returned to their own ship to give their findings. The men were eager to open the door to the cabins below, but the captain, appraising the situation, decided to leave the ship adrift instead. His reasons were based partly on the superstition that a cursed ship remains cursed as does any part of the ship. There have been, in fact, Malachi said, a few cases where parts of cursed ships were repurposed for other vessels that later met similar fates as the originals of their cursed components.

The second reason, Ros asked.

The second reason was a very practical one, Malachi continued, hearing that the door to the quarters below had been chained led the captain to conclude it was a pestilence ship, that some sort of terrible outbreak had occurred and those afflicted had been quarantined. This too wasn't uncommon at that time. A few sick rats on board and that's that. Or some sailor who was less than hygienic on shore leave. And that's the end of the story in the book.

That's very strange, Ros said, Remember that museum we went into, oh, I don't know, somewhere. I can't remember, I think it was the Gulf Coast somewhere?

Oh, yeah, Ros said, It was near Galveston, I think.

That's it. It's just one of those synchronicities. We were down there on the gulf, in this terrible town that was nothing but sprawl, housing developments, and warehouse stores. There was nowhere to walk. Even the waterfront was all privately owned with these houses that varied only in what side the garage was on, Ros laughed, It was dystopic, man. But Ros and I stopped in at this little museum. You know, a tourist trap type of place: lots of signage and pictures, little to show. It was owned by three developers who were out on a fishing trip one day, likely to celebrate their role in the dystopia all around us down there, and Worthington, I think was one guy's name, Leslie or something the other...the third? Do you remember?

I just remember they all wore white hats and shirts and they were very, very sunburned in the pictures.

Anyway, the detail about the chains is what made me think about it again. But it was just a shitty little museum, just the front room of a house, with lots of pictures painted from the account, speculations, and a very long story about how they found the so-called pirate treasures and so on to prop up the paucity of their holdings. So, in the little staple-bound book, that I might add, cost fifteen dollars, the story went like this: they were out fishing and came upon a ghost ship. This was in the 80s sometime. They boarded the boat, and by then everything was pretty corroded and really decayed and already I didn't believe a word of the story. But they said the door to the officer's cabins were chained. And so, they came back with a crowbar, and it didn't take much to pry the rusted chains from the door. Below, they found a large room and lit lamps whose wicks were still moist. The oil, still fresh. All around them were scenes of the gruesome and the fabulous. On a large table, along with the lamp were scientific instruments, dried herbs and minerals. There were glass jars full of crystals and specimens on shelves behind it. There were stuffed animals along the ceiling and walls—birds in flight, tigers, deer, ibex. There were large illuminated books on the table and shelves recessed into the walls. When the men examined one, they found it to be in code. Another written in Latin. And one written in what they decided was Greek. There were trunks of clothes, swords, pistols, and a whole suit of Spanish armor. In one of the trunks, they found, strangely, just brown dust. The papers, or books, or perhaps food that was once there had long crumbled away. They explored the rest of the ship, each cabin in perfect state, as if someone were about to return. One of the men, the sensible one, I guess, got a Coast Guard weather alert on his radio. A storm imminent. They pushed into another room and found a collection of hides that, as one of the men discovered, were all human. They counted fifteen of these skins. By then, the storm was upon them. They got back to their crappy little cigarette boat and sped back to shore. In the morning, hoping to salvage the ship and perhaps bring away treasures, they returned to the coordinates, but, of course, ghost ship had vanished.

Malachi settled back in his chair.

Seemed to me it was just another *Flying Dutchman* tale, Ros said, some ruse like the largest prairie dog in Kansas.

Why do we keep getting taken in by that stuff? Ros asked.

Because we live in the now. Because we still are willing to believe. It's not a bad thing, Ros said.

Yes, but no one has ever recovered anything from the *Flying Dutchman*, Malachi said.

Were there really artifacts from the ship, Ros said. Or was the museum just the three brother's story and a bunch of thrift shop finds?

Oh, there was stuff there. It all seemed hokey though, there was so much. Well, they said that, because if you find treasure, are you really going to tell anyone? Besides, on that day they were suddenly in the middle of a storm, and they were only able to bring back one small souvenir each. They didn't carry back much more because they thought they'd easily be able to go back, more prepared for salvage. Anyway, there was a sabre and scabbard; a leather-bound book that looked to be written in code of some sort possibly an Herbarium or manual from the ship's doctor; and strangely a large crystal bottle sealed with lead and wax that contained yet another small crystal bottle, likewise sealed with lead or silver and inside that, something wrapped in pale leather, red waxed thread, and a small scroll of paper, wound into the roll of leather which looked like it was written in Latin. This was the most interesting to me.

Or Esperanto, Ros said.

Who knows what it said.

Sounds like a reliquary of some sort, I said.

It does, doesn't it, Malachi said.

Do you think it's the same ship, I said.

Well, either that, or these three jokers read the same monograph that I did and based their story on it so to better sell us on their junk, Malachi said. But like Ros, I would rather believe it was. And maybe it's still out there. Sailing in the seas forever. Forever returning to shore. Forever a different appearance.

Ros turned to me and said, Where do you think it is?

I can't believe it ever existed. If it did, it's got to have been reduced to driftwood years ago.

Say it wasn't. Say it's been around and all these stories of encountering the ship on the seas—the *Flying Dutchman* and so on—are true. And imagine this was your ship. Malachi smiled, I find I do this all the time, try to get in the heads of people, things. I'm sure you do this, too. If I were my keys, where would I be? As a detective, Where would I go? What would I do? So, take a shot. Where would you put a ship so that, if you wanted you could visit it every so many decades, like the room in your parent's house?

I thought about it. For some reason, I'd never thought to ask myself if I was so and so. Never put myself in Mann's shoes or any of my other jobs as a detective. I closed my eyes and imagined I was a captain of a ship. Okay, I said, I've sailed for years. I'm immortal for some reason. I needed to return to my ship, but others shouldn't be able to find it. Why do I have to return to the ship? Why am I not just out and about?

I don't know. Maybe it's the key to your immortality somehow. Really, it's just a way to justify that the ship is still in existence somewhere.

Just hanging out in the ocean has worked for a few hundred years until large scale industrial shipping. Something hanging out with sails may stand out. A lake is no good because it's a lake.

Could be a lake, Ros said.

Could be anything, I said. I mean, it's already so ridiculous that sure it is a lake. But, no. For me, I would hide it in plain sight. A restaurant or hotel. A bar maybe.

Like anchored somewhere, a tacky seafood place?

I thought back, and it occurred to me, maybe it was put on wheels and sailed inland. Like the Vikings did and is wrecked somewhere. Or just pulled up on shore and opened for business. They did this in New York. I read once that a lot of the old buildings were ships to begin with. Just slowly building on and building on until, after about a hundred years, no one knows there's a ship right there, in the ground.

That's interesting. That's really interesting, Malachi said, and sat thinking for a moment, forgetting even his cigarette. I keep thinking of these little things I find around the property.

Think it could even be this place, I said.

Yes, could even be this place...Ros said.

Except that Kora had it built for her a little under a hundred years ago, Malachi said. If it weren't for that, I'd be digging the basement up right now. He laughed. No, if it's out there, it's out there somewhere else. Likely near an ocean port or something. I've got to go back and look at my notes. It's got to be somewhere in the Catskills. I've got to go back there.

If you ask me, Ros said, stacking her breakfast dishes, You'll find it anchored near the lost city of Narragonia.

Maybe so, maybe so, Malachi said before standing up and clearing the dishes. I went back to my room and, thinking again about the black credit card, decided to throw away my Everyday Joe clothes, vowing to buy a nice suit, shirt, underclothes, and shoes.

XIII

AND SO WE WERE ON THE ROAD AGAIN: the three of us, dressed in matching coveralls, and the cats in their multi-various coats. Ros and Ros were up front while I was sitting at the table looking over my notebook. It was beginning to seem that there was nothing there. A series of loops that, in the tracery of my thoughts, fed upon themselves and, despite the seeming integrity of intention, fail to connect to anything. Grotto and Cowtail were sitting in my lap, each seeking a new way into my affections. Grotto chewing on the edge of a page, Cowtail on the edge of my hand, and it reminded me of a dream I had the night after Malachi had read to me from Kora's diary. All I could remember by then—and note on a clean page, between Grotto and Cowtail—was that a friend of mine took out her front teeth and said, Ah, now I have six months of not having to wear those things. Then my friend who had given me this assignment pulled out a set of even more teeth, leaned back and said, Tell me about it. Oh, I said in my dream, you're on vacation. And then took out my teeth, which were somewhere in the middle range of the two. And that was it, but it seemed so meaningful.

What do you think of Malachi? Ros called back to me from the front seat, He's far out isn't he? His treasure hunting thing?

I'm just trying to figure that out now, I said.

His ship, this mystery ship of his. It seems to be everywhere, all through time but, you know, somehow it's always about him.

Over and over, Ros said, petting Boots.

Each time we visit, some new detail.

A new detail, and yet the same subject.

An eternal return of an eternal subject of a ship adrift, Ros said.

That could be a song, Ros said. But you know, ol' Malachi isn't all that outside the realm of possibility. Let me ask you, you know what Multiverse Theory is? Ros turned back to me, and Boots leapt down and then started cleaning his ears at my feet.

Not beyond what it sounds like, I said.

It's a start, but the real questions are: does it exist and why? I mean, we've all thought about different worlds. Pick up any book, watch a few movies, and you'll find a different universe. Or how about our dreams? What are dreams? Ever think that maybe dreams are an empirical conduit to another world? Ros asked.

What is this? The middle ages? Dreams are just the processing of daily experiences and anxieties, Ros said.

What is this, the early 20th century? Or maybe that's not all they are, ok? So, this brings us to the uncertainty principle. Let's say dreams are nothing except the processing of unconscious information of the day? But what is that information? We know the body edits our reality—stick a pin in your toe and you feel it and see it at the same time, but that doesn't really happen at the same time because it takes time for the nerves to send a signal to the brain, for the brain to figure out what it means, and to send information back down. So, what if the multiverse, like a particle, is both there and not at the same time, and that part of us is perceiving it, but to keep us from going crazy, the brain edits it out, or maybe selects what is real. The idea of multiverse, Ros, is that it is both, and then both again. A popular view is that from every choice we are confronted with, every possibility plays out in a strafe of time. Materially, it is that a photon can be a wave and a particle at the same time, that they exist in two places at once and then stabilize...maybe they choose to stabilize, or there is a tendency to stabilize or present as a particle again. Or it's that we do.

I like to think of things like that, past lives, and so on, but I always feel it is totally delusional. Why is everyone a reincarnation of a prince or princess, I said.

Thank you, the other Ros said. Who is the origin point for all this? You? Me? Whose choices are changing the world?

Oh, isn't it all about what am I going to wear to the ball?

Not in the least, Ros said.

Time is a container, but imposed, a way to sort ourselves accordingly. Nouns of a verb. Time then exists outside of ourselves, that time is a thing we are subject to. But time is perceived differently by people, and by single people throughout the day, yet we have a clock, we look at the clock, which itself is understood to represent something like time, but it is a cheating aesthetic choice, every four years we have to catch up on the unsightly time left over by the clocks. They cannot contain time, it spills over. Time itself is essentially human, and maybe even urban humans. Humans are subject to other humans and time is the currency. Time is an unoccupied mask.

But we do grow old, Ros said.

Yes, we are born and grow old and die. And time is a way to account for this, but how paradoxical is this idea of birth and death. If we are brought into life, why leave? And if we leave, why arrive? The day comes and goes. People come and go, and time is a myth that allows us to order this, if not explain it in a mythic sense, to comfort as a kind of explanation. Perception contradicts itself, oh, it was a long time ago, I can say. Time is just a measurement in the movement between two types of matter. Anything can be called time. So many suns, moons, and cups of coffee. And even if you say you remember, what? You could have some sort of major brain fart and think you're doing something for the first time, or that you are doing it all over again, or play piano or violin and have no memory of knowing how. I'm Ros. There are other Roses. Not reincarnated. Not moving through time, but Ros. The same Ros because this idea of individual Ros is an idea of time, accounting for the movements between Ros and Ros.

Anyway, Ros said, what if they all were? And what if they were all each other and remember themselves from these different incarnations. Besides, of course, something that depends on human perception will necessarily be from the human perspective. We are the ones sitting here thinking about it.

Traveling down the road, aren't we? We've always told ourselves tales. The best definition of myth is a resolution of a contradiction, Ros said.

Yes, that's a good one. Myth, however, does more than that, Ros said. We act under unobserved, although always observed circumstances, right? I know you've told me as much. Just as we are under the influence of time, of electromagnetism, of just the body's metabolism when making a decision, she said.

Ros started drumming on the steering wheel.

I can't say I buy it, I said.

Well, if you got the money, honey, I got the time, Ros said.

Exactly, Ros said, it's made in the minds of those who accept it, and these stories only serve to recreate that reality and perpetuate that reality.

Maddox leapt on the counter and was slowly pushing a cup towards the edge, inch by amusing inch. Down, I shouted, but only served to catch the cup before it hit the floor. Maddox let a paw hang off the edge. Grotto and Cowtail, however, erupted from my lap, using my thighs as respective launching pads.

What? Ros said from the front.

Clowns. Yes, Ros, said, Clowns are precisely those in whom the virtual does not register. Give them a gun, it falls apart. Starve them, they eat a shoe. If there ever is a robot apocalypse, some clown will be mopping the floor and accidentally unplug our computer overlords.

Cowtail and Grotto, likewise challenged, it seemed, by the appearance of Maddox on the counter, had decided to climb the tapestry curtain separating the bedroom from the common room and, having come to their senses, were slowly descending the tapestry curtain backwards and each slow backwards step was punctuated by the sound of popping fabric.

Is it alright if I make coffee? I said.

Sure, Ros said. Make enough for the whole crew, will you?

Right. And in quantum physics, there are unseen influences, it seems, from the strange behavior of particles in the quantum realm. Say it is a fifth or sixth dimension that we can't see, and these strange behaviors don't make sense to us because of our ability to see only a limited number of dimensions.

In the clown dimension, is it a hat, is it an elephant in a snake?

Or just a drawing in a book. Or words on a page? But it is still there, she said.

Either way, the clown will mistake it or turn it into a boat and float it downstream.

A mystery ship, I said.

But can it be described in math? Proofed?

We made up math. When we couldn't figure something out, we made up a math that would, Ros said. We make up experiments to resolve these contradictions. Calculus, imaginary numbers. Fractals. And still ignore that there are sand paintings that represent the same mathematical principles, and then, once completed, they slowly blow away, erased by the same forces that the image graphs. Myth provides a similar function. It resolves contradictions through metaphors, through analogies. Perhaps, we do perceive that extra dimension? Perhaps it is myth and story. Maybe it is art? Language?

Maybe it is anything, he said. If I say that when my foot hurts it means it will rain and then it rains? I make the syllogistic correlative that pain in my foot makes it rain, and as long as I want it to not rain, I take care of my foot, and if I need it to rain, I hit it with a hammer.

That's sympathetic magic, Ros said, not myth.

It resolves a contradiction.

No, it justifies self-harm.

The coffee pot was surprisingly efficient. I opened the refrigerator and took out the small carton of cream and discretely poured some on a saucer for Maddox, Cowtail, and Grotto in turn. Helmut and Croll appeared, too, and a few slaps of the paw occurred between them and in the tumult I saw that I was surrounded. Maillon and Boots appeared, rubbing against my leg. I poured more on the first saucer and offered another, thinking that four to one, three to the other would be an okay set up, each head in each cardinal direction, but they moved from competing over one saucer, then the next, in turn, not heeding anything cardinal, or perhaps all avoiding some invisible presence. Headlamp was the only one missing. I'd nearly forgotten there was coffee.

Cream? I shouted to the Roses.

Exactly, dreams.

Dreams?

Why do we discount the individual if they dream they are flying. Or their teeth fall out.

Or are simply taken out for vacation, I said handing them coffee. There's cream in this?

I can take it if you don't want it, I said.

Would you?

No problem, I said.

I'm okay with cream, Ros said.

I'll be right back, I said.

As I was carefully pouring another cup of coffee, I noticed the cats had licked one saucer upside down, and a few were at odds trying to nose underneath it for the slim possibility of cream. It was there once, I thought, why wouldn't it be there again. That seemed sound to me. The other saucer had been licked under the couch.

The world is a nutshell full of bad dreams, Ros said.

Coffee, I said.

Well, not all bad, Ros said. Thanks.

Wow, I said, I hadn't noticed the sun go down. Can't believe I missed the sunset.

Well, if we speed up to about 1,060 miles per hour, we could catch up with it, if you wanted, then I could ease up on the pedal and keep it right there just almost below the horizon, but then we'd only enjoy it for, let's see, it would take us about an hour to catch up with it, then, yeah, about five, ten minutes before we'd hit water.

The mountains kind of cut it short, Ros said.

I didn't think of that, I said.

We are on the dark side of the earth.

I went back to the couch and my notebook. I'd set the coffee down in one of the recessed cup spaces, but it had still spilled a little on the table and down the leg. There was no trace of it on the ground or about midway up the table leg. Maddox came up and rubbed on my leg. Oh, I said, Now you want some love? Do you want love? Come here, come get some loving. I picked him up, and he twisted out of my arms.

What about love?

Love is another sense. Yet the epistemological mistake is the same: that it detects a singularity, Ros said.

I think; therefore, I am.

I think in the environment of my thoughts; therefore, I am as much as I am in relationship to my environment.

Maddox returned to just rubbing on my legs, even after I sat down on the couch to finally have my coffee. There was hair in it.

I think in the middle of my dream; therefore, I am dreaming my thinking.

Shouldn't dreams be considered in the empirical formulation of reality?

They can't be repeated, Ros said. They aren't scientific.

Or we don't know yet the variables because we discount them as anything but real. Yet, when you dream about infidelity, aren't you jealous? If perception is related to metabolism, doesn't that rush of adrenalin affect your reality, the decisions you make, the path you take and the reality you create?

Well, I might wake up aroused. So you think dreams are a portal of discovery to other dimensions? Are we back in ancient Rome?

No. I don't believe they are portals. I think they are a creative rendering of non-linguistically recognized sensory data rendered into the language that is available. I think art is the representation.

Art is representational, imagine that.

Art. Even Newton thought that art described the world. He read *Ovid* as an alchemical manual.

Newton also believed that the world would end in 2060.

Well... Ros said.

So how do you go from this, inter-dimensional art, to other worlds? I see how it maybe supports quantum being.

Art is the iron shavings seen from above, moving mysteriously and of its own. We can't see the magnet below.

In that case, if we take all of art as a point and place these points on a field and in this way compile a data spread, would we find a picture there? What would it look like? Would we see into this other dimension?

Maybe. Maybe we already have. Maybe that is what art already does? Like dreaming, perhaps, art already aggregates a data set and renders it visually. Maybe fractal geometry is a very basic revelation of what the mind does intuitively.

Or, is it the mind that is ordering it all?

What if you are both right? I said. Just two perceptions of the same object?

Like particles, we can be both, Ros said.

Ros is Ros, and Ros is Ros, but Roses are different, I said.

As a wise person once said: stories is everything, and everything is stories, Ros said.

XIV

IT WAS LATE. The somnolent running lights were on inside the RV, and the conversation had quieted, not that it was missed. The cats seemed to have likewise retired to their various sleeping spots.

We've cleared out the Granny Attic for you if you're feeling sleepy, Ros said, tapping the roof above him. When we were clearing it out earlier, it turned out that was Headlamp's hiding place. It was full of his fur. I kind of hated to disturb it—it was like a sculpture. Beautiful. I kept it all and maybe I'll do something with it.

Thank you. Send my apologies to Headlamp.

Will do. But I'm sure you'll have the opportunity shortly. A cat's spot is a cat's spot. Oh, and here. He handed me a light on a head strap. Maybe you'll blend in, he said, but, in case you want to read or something—there's no light up in there. And, you're free to read anything on the shelves.

Or any book on the floors, Ros said. They seem to find their way there.

I took the headlamp and finding no other way up, used the counter top, drew aside the curtain, and then kind of threw my weight up into the space above the cockpit of the RV. Ros or Ros had made the space quite nice. There were pillows and an egg crate foam top and two blankets—a light cotton sheet and a heavier quilt. I settled in, but felt something lumpy, and extracted Kora Derringer's diary from one of the side pockets of the coveralls. I'd put it there to return to Malachi at breakfast but gotten so involved with the conversation that I'd forgotten to give it to him. Suddenly there was a large tail in my face. Headlamp had come to claim his spot. I gave his cheeks a little roughing, then smoothed the fur on his back. He settled in on my chest, and I was surprised by his weight. There wasn't much else to do, so I switched on the headlamp, pulled the curtain, and found where Malachi had left off:

...We, Madam Van Valsing, the Viscount, and I, decided to picnic that day and went north to the beautiful lake that nestled hidden at the edge of this little hayseed town full of impoverished homesteads, tow headed children, and sorrowful women wearing their fingers raw trying to guide those children away from various perils of country living. A very spiritual place, a place full of spirits Madam Van Valsing said. The Viscount just walked, carrying the basket as if he were just an automaton and all the while I hoped his spring would wind down and I could take the basket and be alone with Van Valsing and we would walk down the shore and have a very pleasant day of it, but as I was thinking this, we were presently at the shore and Madam pointed out where we were all to sit. She acted fragile, though in this very young summer light, she had smooth skin, rosy cheeks and the blunt features of a child. I wondered how she had traveled, if the Viscount were to be believed, to so many lands and seen so many things—she must be older than me and perhaps even the Viscount, and later I discussed this with L. and he said that her type was difficult to tell the age of, that he had met a woman who worked in the little hotel he stayed at in Greece and each time he saw her, he figured her to be the proprietor's daughter and would be very condescending to her, often offering shreds of, what he as a young imperious man himself, not yet twenty-one, considered already sage and aged wizened advice, only to find, as he was leaving, that she was the proprietor's wife. Had he known, he started, and simply began laughing and as I pressed him for what he was going to say, he blushed and responded, well, you see, Kora, one cannot tell the age of magi so easily.

After a spot had been selected, the Viscount shook out an oddly rough blanket with transitioning shades of color, from burgundy to midnight blue, and we all sat there while he laid out the lunch. It was to be a picnic of apples, a soft Norwegian cheese—I can't remember if it was from a goat or cow but it was delicious cheese and smoked oysters, and a very good baguette. There was also dandelion wine and when I pointed out how cloudy it was, the pair, the Viscount and Van Valsing both laughed, and said, it was the way of dandelion wine to go through periods of cloudiness and clarity, like we ourselves or as if the flowers have forgotten that they have left the earth. And we drank and ate and it was very good and when we were done, the Viscount said, like Thoreau, he would be very pleased to simply build a provisional shanty and stay at the water's edge for a year or so, learning as much as he could about the things around him. I thought this a thoroughly vapid statement and looked to Van Valsing to see what she thought but couldn't penetrate her very fine features and couldn't probe her eyes too long without my own watering and having to look away, but finally, fueled by his dumb pronouncement, the Viscount decided he wanted to walk the perimeter of the lake.

Van Valsing poured me another glass of wine as the day was entering into dusk, and the lake seemed to take on some of the approaching twilight's character and I looked very long into my glass and was startled when I heard and felt Van Valsing talking: Many years ago, I came here to visit three little girls who lived right there, across the lake from us, you see the house there? I looked, but all I saw was scattered brush, a darkened patch of earth by the water's edge, a small overgrown pile of brick near the tree line. There you see? The house is warm, the chimney has smoke, there is light flickering in the windows as the three girls stare out to the woods. Their names were Eurydice, Diana, and Poppy. I laughed then and excused myself, but Van Valsing answered, Yes, from high to low, it seems they have run out of steam in naming girls. But, they were special girls, very special. These sisters, because they had no parents and because their grandmother could no longer do the house work, tend the field, or hunt for food, they did this work. Eurydice tended the garden. Poppy took care of the house and the grandmother. And Diana went out and hunted for their meat. One day, each sister tended to her chores, but at sunset, when they gathered in their small hut for dinner, Eurydice had not returned from the field. Diana, who was by then a great hunter, went out to the field with a taper and shield to search for her sister. When she returned, she said that the field had been tended that day, that there was a basket full of vegetables for dinner, but that her sister's footprints led away from the basket, until, strangely, they suddenly disappeared, as if swallowed by the earth. The grandmother, swore, if I were not so old, I would have been in the field and would have my grave set so that my granddaughters would not have to dig it themselves. The next day Diana hunted at dawn, tended to the field at midday, and searched for Eurydice before dinner. Poppy and her grandmother waited at the table for Diana, but she did not return that night or the next morning. The grandmother lamented, oh if I were not so old, I would have been out hunting and met a wolf and been its dinner, and my sweet granddaughters would not have to worry over my corpse. The only sister left, Poppy tended to her grandmother in the mornings, then set traps for game before she tended the field in the afternoon and checked the traps before dinner when she would return, cook, and give the grandmother her potion to ease her pains. One day, however, Poppy tended to her new chores as she had before, but that evening she found a foot in one of the traps. The sole of the foot was blackened and hard, the flesh laced with delicate purple veins, and the nails were thick, yellowed, and streaked. She buried this foot and hurried home. That night her grandmother would not get out of bed and forewent dinner. The next day Poppy tended to her chores and this time found a thick ball of grey hair in the brambles at the edges of their little field. She made a small fire and burned the hair. When she returned that night, her grandmother had covered her head with the sheets and again refused to eat or get out of bed. The next day, Poppy tended to her chores as usual. This time there was no foot in the trap but a fat rabbit. There was no hair in the brambles, but clusters of juicy berries. And when she returned home, her grandmother was out of bed, and wearing her nice dress, with a dapper hat on her head. Poppy set the table and prepared the meal. The grandmother, however, although seeming so well, refused again to eat. The next morning, a beautiful young woman, wearing a nice dress and dapper hat left the small hut, locked the door and was not seen again. Sometime later, a neighbor whose well had gone dry, decided that the well near the abandoned hut might hold water. He tossed his bucket down three times and each time pulled up the bones of each of the daughters. Do you understand the story, my dear Kora?

We sat in silence for a while as the sun was setting and I was lost in thinking about the story, wondering which of the sisters I was until Madam Van Valsing smiled and continued: even where I was, in the East studying with the Sages, one could feel the great dragon had stirred just a little in her rest. You see, just in those trees all around us, there were rows and columns of the most mysterious apples ever grown. And they were carried by foot across continents of ice, in sacks in the shallow bows of boats, along with the people, the people from the forests, from the plains, from the seas of Atlantis. It was said the apples grew on trees of silver and were tended by a man and woman who knew any language that was spoken to them. It is also said that the man and woman were the same person—it was according to the observer, how the figure manifested. When asked how they got there, they replied that they walked from the south, for years and years they walked, until, finding no reason to walk any farther. Now only a few arches and grottos exist in the woods.

Just then, at the conclusion of Madam Van Valsing's story, a number of fiery orbs shot out across the surface of the lake, as if they were a coordinated row of aquabatic swimmers bathed in brilliant colors. Van Valsing took my hands and I joyously took hers. Look, she said, look, there they are! The spirits of this lake, they dance for you! They greet you! Such a rare event! Kora, they have indeed blessed us, blessed our meeting and friendship. I was nearing tears, and wanted so to join myself with her as the orbs had joined themselves in the waters, and imagine their shining presence now below the surface, dancing at the lake's enchanted depths, and from my own depths intense varicolored blazes, but it was then, on the very edge of combustion that the Viscount, disheveled and out of breath arrived from the opposite direction of his departure asking stupidly, did I miss something? They came, dear Viscount, the spirits of the lakes. I pointed out a small burn on his shirt. Oh, I must have been clumsy; my cigarette holder is a treasure, but a little worn out and cannot keep hold of these new cigarettes for its life. They fall out, you see, like this one, onto my clothes. I must replace it soon. Indeed, you must, I said, but I imagine your shirt maker will be displeased if you do. He smiled a toothy and somewhat false smile. I've always admired those with titles, and yet I wondered wherever he received his. Nevertheless, when we returned, I made a gift of an ivory and lapis cigarette holder, which he graciously accepted and immediately implemented.

That night, I brazenly mentioned that Madam Van Valsing and the Viscount should stay with me at my home, as permanent guests, and to this they demurred and laughed, saving me my brashness and embarrassment. But before they left, Van Valsing intimated that we were now spiritual sisters and that, it was only on this fact that she even mentioned it, because of the political unrest in her country, she was unable to pay for her and the Viscount's travel and lodging. I kissed her, and said, dear sister, send every and all your bills to me. She said she couldn't, and explained that she was only lamenting the fact, and apologized for speaking of politics at all. But I insisted and she accepted with the softest ever kiss on my hand. Then their valet and driver announced that the car was ready. Write, I called out, but received only a parting wave in reply. It was then that I vowed that I would always support her and would immortalize her life in a novel and have just now prepared and will set to that very task this very minute.

Tired, I adjusted Headlamp and my own headlamp and opened my notebook. I drew the lake from Kora's diary in Kora's own violet ink. Then I added Malachi's ship to the drawing. On a fresh page I decided to write an original epic poem to the cats but could only get through twelve verses until I ran out of words that rhymed with cat. Again, I tried to find the directions of influences and again it became a scramble of feedback, and it seemed, suddenly that I had written Kora's name somewhere earlier, or messed up copying this iteration of the map, but I didn't have a chance to find out before Headlamp moved up more on my chest and pushed his face into mine. I shifted the notebook above his head and pressed it against the ceiling and wished then that I had a space pen and maybe binder clips. I shifted a little and suffered Headlamp's claws but managed to adjust enough to turn to a new page, and rather than putting Mann in the center, as I have with all of the other tangled maps, I wrote my name and then the name of my friend, and then the various clues and influences, and for a moment it all seemed to connect and the constellation around me became clear, and for a moment my head was whirling until I realized that, of course, it would all connect to me because I was the center of the map because I had moved through it all alone, the motor of the orrery, more or less. I made a note of this, put the notebook away, scratched Headlamp under the chin, and fell asleep in the warm, humming confines of the granny attic.

XV

WHEN I RETURNED HOME I found that I'd lost my apartment, my possessions and what jobs I had. I've since been sleeping in Golden Gate Park and spending my days in North Beach. My original notebook and my wallet were gone when I woke up on a pier by a pile of seals, but miraculously somehow I still had the fountain pen. Since then, I'd tried to reconstruct everything from the notebook on various scraps of paper and then in a new notebook I'd stolen from an art store on Market Street. Soon, however, I gave up and devoted the pages to mapping out all the fruit and nut trees in San Francisco, as well as, developing a calendar for when grocery stores dumped their food. But mostly, I spent my days sitting on a bench in Washington Park, and it was on one of those days, that a woman in a tulip dress sat next to me and introduced herself as Mauve. She then asked if I my name was Guy.

Yes, I said.

Good, she said, Now listen, I'm going to tell you a little story: Once upon a time, there was a girl who had three brothers. Of the four children, their mother loved her three sons the most. If the sons wanted chocolate to drink, they got chocolate. If they wanted to go swim in the river, they swam in the river. If they wanted to spend all day out hunting with their dogs, they spent all day hunting with their dogs. The girl, however, could not—for she was too busy grinding and boiling the chocolate. She was too busy gathering and washing clothes at the river then drying them on rocks. She was too busy feeding the dogs and cleaning and cooking the game. On top of all of this, she was given a blunt knife to carry out her last task.

But the girl had an admirer. This admirer was an alchemist named Seolfurus. Each day when she went to grind the chocolate, the alchemist would produce a cauldron of the finest ever tasted. When she went to wash the clothes, the alchemist gave her a powder and mechanism that eased the task. And when she had to clean and cook the game, the alchemist brought her a crown of flowers, gave her a knife, whose marbled blade had been sharpened by acids and was sharper than any she'd held, and made for her a winter coat from the hides of hinds and hares.

For a time no one noticed that she was accomplishing these tasks with speed and ease. But soon enough they took notice and would see her reading when before she would be at the mortar and pestle. She would be drawing by the water when before she would be scrubbing her brother's embroidered doublets. And when she should be covered in blood and ash, she was looking at maps of the world. It couldn't be explained. Even when the daughter was given more work.

One day the mother found the coat and knife. She bid her youngest son to take the knife and wearing the coat, go about as if he were his sister and do her chores. The boy did as he was told and dressed as his sister and went to the river to do the wash. The alchemist went to visit the girl, but when it was revealed that it was the little brother, it was too late. The knife was already in the alchemist's belly, the blood already covering the boy's hand. Shaken by what he had done, the boy dropped the knife, shed the coat, and ran home.

The girl, unaware of the plot, by then had arrived at the river to do her chores, only to find the alchemist dying at the edge of the water. The alchemist asked the girl to bring chocolate to drink, and this she did. Then the alchemist asked the girl to wash the bloody coat, and this she did. Finally, she was asked to skin the alchemist and make a fine suit from the hide. And this she did.

The girl, dressed in the alchemist's flesh, returned home with the fine knife and first cut off the hands of her little brother. Then she cut off the feet of her middle brother. Then she cut off the head of the oldest brother. These she cooked all together in a pot with chocolate and then fed to her mother and two remaining brothers. After this stew was finished, she cut off the head of her mother, buried her brothers in a well, and lived happily ever after. The end.

She waited for a response. I sat there.

Do you understand? she said.

No, I said. I don't understand any of it.

That's ok, she said and got up and left. I sat there, by the guano-streaked statue of Benjamin Franklin and thought about the past year. The coveralls were still covered in cat hair. I put my head in my hands and pressed them into my eyes. There was a bright explosion, like the birth of a star, then a shattering of that light into a galaxy of small darting sparks, and it made me think of a place— if there was a place among the heavens—just past the ruins of the Sutro Baths where it is possible to scale down a slope near where the walls have fallen away and where the drains were to empty and then, after climbing near a patch of rosemary, hop from one boulder to the next, so that soon one is standing on a large stone surrounded by the Pacific Ocean, and from there watch the sun set over the ocean, prolonging the day as much as possible, and from there watch the orange flash against midnight blue on the choppy waters like a tapestry fluttering in the wind and know that these last rays of light are the last rays of light to be seen from that edge of coast, that sitting there you are on the edge of that earth moving into night. Returning, however, is more difficult, if you mis-time the tide, and are fumbling in the dark, it is easy to end up with wet shoes, socks, and trousers, so it is only occasionally that I go there and watch the end of one day, as if it were the end of all days, and it is only when I feel like the sole inhabitant of a small and autonomous world and I need to unknot something, before I return to this other world, one tilted by the night, or stay there, stranded.

SWERVE FIVE

VI

HERE'S WHERE THE STORY TAKES A DETOUR. Thelma puts her hands on my forehead and immediately I feel a release. This isn't something you should consider doing on your own, she says, and I'm quick to agree. Outside, I can see the sun rippling through the trees, bright orange slithering between bits of green, and I think back to my days as a young man in Ojai, to the hot springs there and the woman I was supposed to meet after finding the case with the bells.

That will happen next year, she says, and the year after that. In the meantime, I need you to focus on the here and now.

I am, I say. I'm trying. But how did I get here? I was just in San Francisco.

Did you look at a clock while you were there? Remember what I told you about clocks.

I don't remember, I say. What do I do now?

You were looking for a woman, remember? And this woman you are looking for is looking for a man who is himself looking for another man who, in turn, is looking for himself. Do you understand what I'm trying to tell you?

I don't think so.

She sighs and shakes her head. She lifts a small glass vial from her apron pocket. It's stoppered with a cork and labeled *Summer Suicides*.

I think this might explain things, she says, holding it under my nose.

And soon I think I understand. It's like a story I've heard a thousand times—light bending around corners, spectral lines dancing near a woman floating in aether, men with mirrors measuring her longitudinal libration.

A detective leaning forward, questioning a little mermaid girl sitting at a kitchen table, the one whose name was Bayou.

I leaned forward and pressing the record button on my contraption, I held out the microphone to little Bayou. I was asking about Aquifer.

Can you tell me what you saw that day?

Bayou swallowed over the cherry pitted anxiety that now lived in her throat and nodded.

It was dark, she said, and there were so many shadows. I'd gone down to the kitchen to see about some water.

She's always seeing about some water, offered The Woman of the Spring, hovering, trying to make things right again.

I gave her a look, and the woman retreated, a moray eel of maternal anxiety.

Go on, I prompted, and the girl nodded.

It was dark when I came down the stairs, but I smelled something when I reached the landing. A flower. And I stopped there just. I breathed it in. And then I heard a crash in the kitchen. Then a few words spoken softly. And then Guy started screaming.

You're sure it was Guy?

Bayou frowned. Of course I'm sure. Who else could it have been? And then I ran toward the noise. When I got to the kitchen, Selkie was bleeding. There was a gash in her thigh. I thought Guy had...I thought he had...well never mind what I thought. He wasn't there, though. He was nowhere I could see. Bayou shook her head and continued: It was only later, when I heard about the garden that I understood what must have happened.

And what's that? I— the detective asked, our voice stretched tense as tightropes of bubble gum.

Well. Little Bayou looked up at The Woman of the Spring. Selkie killed him. She must have. She stabbed him in the kitchen, no, in the gut, but while they were in the kitchen. And then he stumbled out to the yard and died in that patch of zucchini flowers right out there. What else could have happened?

Fauve, beside me now, bending light like nobody's business, leaned forward and pushed a lock of platinum hair behind her ear.

What was the flower?

Excuse me?

The flower, Fauve explained. The one you smelled on the landing.

Oh that, Bayou said, quickly shifting in her seat, a look of relief egg-washing her cheeks. I want to say jasmine?

You're sure?

No. Not sure. But probably jasmine. Yes...yes, it wasdefinitely jasmine.

Fauve wrote something down on a notepad. When she'd finished, she lowered her voice and shook her head. You can't get stuck in a void, she said. People don't know that. They think you can get lost in there, in those pockets of light, in those fields of flowers, but even with everything moving away from us, red-shifting like it is, getting stretched, even with all that, it's impossible to get lost.

I nodded and turned back at the girl. She shifted in her mermaid costume and ran a thumb over a kneecap sharp as a shard of sequined glass.

Fauve and I looked at one another. Very interesting.

This was four years to the day before the Madri-Gals would vanish for good.

VII

I'M STOPPING IN AT A DINER in Central California, a bunch of RV's parked outside. I'm looking to indulge in a nice stack of flapjacks with some warm maple syrup, and that's when I see the guy—my mark from out in San Francisco. The weird thing is that when I first see him, I think it's Ros, the Slim Jim guy from the bus. He's wearing overalls and has a distant look in his eye like his little grey cells have hung up a "Gone Fishing" sign. But he's wearing the Bird of Paradise in his lapel, so I know it's him. When he nears my booth, I raise a hand in awkward greeting, and I notice he looks relieved to see me.

You're gonna need this, he says, slipping a book onto my table. *Avalanche*, it's called. Something about the book feels familiar. Got time for some flapjacks? I ask, but he doesn't. He doesn't have time for much of anything anymore, he says, and then he turns to go. But before he's made it to the door, he doubles back, brandishing a manila envelope. Almost forgot! Expense receipts! He frisbees the envelope to me and then hightails it out of the diner. When he's gone I have a look at the book. *Avalanche* by Caroline Mints. I open it up and that's when I see the name of the publisher: *Fauve of the Spring Publishing.* Big Sur, California. I slip it into my bag and head to the car. Looks like I'm going to Big Sur. When I get in the car something makes me open the manila envelope. Inside it there are no receipts. Instead it's filled with the fur of at least half a dozen different cats.

The publishing house is just that, a house. A lilac Victorian with a small pond in the yard. A man greets me and says they gave up the press long ago, but I'm welcome to go up to the attic and look through their archives. When I ask about the name, when I ask about Fauve, he shrugs.

One of our authors came up with that, he says. Clinnamen, do you know his work? Of course we didn't do his early stuff, not *Magnets and Madrigals*, nothing so prestigious, but his later books were all ours. Too esoteric for the mainstream set.

His wife takes me up to the attic, and offers me a fish sandwich which I gratefully accept. Boxes line the shelves. In the corner stands a mannequin wearing a black and white daisy dress.

I'd start with these, the woman says, handing me two very old letters. I take a seat on the floor. As I begin reading, a small blue beetle scurries across the floor and perches on the toe of my boot.

October 1, 1816

Dearest sister,

To think that you might read this without me sitting at your side pains me to no end. It has been a fortnight since I left you at the station, and had I known then what I know now, I would have clung to your side like the evening moss that drips from the side of the ice house down where we used to play as girls. You a soldier and I a rosy-cheeked novitiate about to take her vows.

The manor is not at all what I was led to expect. It looms four stories, slick with green-tinged stones. Windows peer out from it like hundreds of eyes and sometimes it seems to me the labyrinthine twisting of its halls are meant to resemble the needled feet of a millipede. Sometimes I think that while I sleep the halls change position, that the whole manor folds in upon itself, swallowing me whole each night only to spit me forth in the morning like a newly born grub, blind and chewing at the walls of her world for some taste of reality.

The man of the house is frightening, and his mother not much better. It is said that once he had a sister, beautiful beyond all imagining with blond hair that fell in ringlets to her waist and eyes like the sun

*sinking into whirlpools of fresh blue ocean water. I've come to under-
stand that something terrible happened to her. She's gone now, but
they speak of her as if she's not gone at all, but has simply wandered
out into the oak grove and down into the pond, where the water lilies
lounge like there's no tomorrow, to disappear.*

*There is a portrait of her in the hallway near the master's study. I
say that the portrait is of her, but there's no way of telling. It is of a
small boy and girl holding hands. Blond, and dressed in purple velvet,
the boy is clearly the master, but the girl beside him, whose hand he
grasps as if he thinks she might try to escape, she is turned away from
the viewer. What she stares at in the mountains behind her, I cannot
say. But something must have held her fancy back there because she's
turned so thoroughly that one gets the feeling that there never was
more to her than the back of a head, golden as late afternoon sunshine.
In the girl's other hand, she holds a brass key, a red ribbon wound
round its bow. Yesterday Cook caught me staring at the portrait, and
narrowing her eyes, she shook her head.*

"We're not supposed to look at that," she said, and when I inquired
further, she'd speak no more of the matter except to say: "Some
things aren't meant for this earth. And our mistress, she was one of
those things."

She'd speak no more after that, and if I'm not mistaken, she went
pale except for small patches just beneath her eyes that bloomed
red as cherries driven into a white tablecloth by the heel of a t
emperamental palm.

October 10, 1816

My dearest sister,

*I've just returned to my chamber and as I sit down to write you, I find
that my hand shakes almost uncontrollably and my breath still comes
in fits and starts. I hardly know what to make of what I've just seen.*

It was dusk and I'd gone for a stroll with Timothy and Elizabeth. I let them wander out toward the moors in the hopes that they would run off some of their copious energy, that I might not have to work so hard to calm them when night fell. I had set a blanket on the cool, wet grass and was going to occupy myself with some needlepoint when I saw a glimmer of something between the trees out in the oak grove. Without thinking, I set down my work and stood up, walking in the direction of the flash. I should have known at once, as soon as I entered that gloomy copse, that something was amiss, but it was as if I were overtaken by a curious compulsion to proceed despite my better judgment. I walked almost as if in a dream, down a dirt path overgrown with venous-blue hydrangeas, and then past a brook, and down to a bright green glen, at the center of which lay a stark white fairy ring of bulbous mushrooms. The kind I'm always warning the children against.

I shall never know what spirit overtook me, but I soon found myself at the center of that ring. I closed my eyes for but a second and in that second I knew worlds beyond our own. I knew the full capacity of space, of time, of the straining impotence of human potential—a truth, I'm afraid to say, both frightening and disheartening.

When I opened my eyes again, it was the deepest night and standing before me were a woman and a small girl. The woman held a lantern, and in its warming glow, I observed her pallid skin, her sharp features, her blue eyes like vessels sunk in a shipwreck graveyard. It was her. I was certain of it. It was the one they talk about. She didn't speak, but in those shipwrecked eyes I saw the full horror of her existence, of the misdeeds that had come before and of the misery that still lay ahead. At her side, the child frowned up at me. She had a strange way about her, and her features were more like the master's than could have been expected. She wore a little black bonnet on her flaxen head, and a dress that looked like moonlight carved out of moss. It hung from her straight to the earth where it seemed almost to mingle and become one with it.

I asked their names, but the woman only shook her head, and the girl held up a hand to stop me. On her palm I observed a small birthmark and a finely demarcated X. Something about that mark plunged me back into reality and with horror I realized that Timothy and Eliza-beth had been unattended for some time, and given the position of the moon in the sky, I guessed that it had been some hours at least. Spurred, I turned and ran up the hill and back toward the manor.

The moors were still, lifeless, so I hurried back to the house, my skirt catching on a bramble and tearing. I didn't stop. I ran until, breath-less, I reached the front door. There stood the children. Wet from what must have been a passing thunderstorm to which I bore no witness, the children were shivering, glassy-eyed and pale. I took them into my arms but they hardly seemed to see me. Elizabeth in particular struck my heart clean through with worry, for no matter how thoroughly I shook her or how loudly I called her name, she simply stared straight ahead, unseeing.

"What's wrong with her?" I demanded of Timothy.

"She saw her," he said, his voice shaking from more than just the cold. "She saw Fauve."

VIII

I SET THE LETTERS DOWN AND RUB MY TEMPLE. There's a pain starting up there like tiny snakes balling together and writhing just below the surface of the skin. The woman returns with more fish sandwiches. This time she slips a little whiskey into the tea and I give her an appreciative wink.

I think you'll find this one interesting. She hands me a sheet of paper on which two separate paragraphs are written, each composed in a different hand.

Excerpted from the work of C.K. SYVARGENTUS

The Old Ones named it The River at The End of the World, and some-times when the wind is low and the pounding rains ceases for more than a moment, the stars will come out to drip down and shimmer against its blue-green surface, and the notion can almost be believed. But most days it is just the far end of the Crooked River, and it opens onto a lonesome stretch of water that eventually leads out to the open, frozen sea. It is from this frozen sea that the liniments must be gath-ered so that the proper expulsion might take place. Let's begin:

What you will need:
-the tears of ten women
-empty serving dishes
-palm fronds
-eucalyptus leaves
-unction

(The remainder of the fragment is unreadable.)

My Dearest DG,

As I read through the case file on the Clinnamen Affair, I keep thinking back to this one night with Thelma. We went out by the knoll. We lay down under the telephone wires. We stared up at them.

Imagine white sheets hanging from those wires. A dozen at least, she'd said.

I thought she was crazy, but I did what she said.

Do you see them there? she whispered. See them hanging in the breeze? Bright white against the night. And she snapped her teeth when she said it like she was biting down on something, snapping off the head of a small animal, a violent rending.

I didn't see them there. I didn't, but I lied and I said that I did. And then she grabbed my hand and she looked over and smiled at me.

Good, she said, a look of absolute calm on her face.

I wish I hadn't lied to her now. I wish to God I hadn't lied.

This last fragment is unsigned, and though it's clearly addressed to me, I have no idea what to make of it. The fact that it concerns Thelma makes me feel uneasy. I frown and fold the paper in half. Then into quarters. I have to leave, I say, and then I drink the rest of my tea and sit by the window for the remainder of the day. Around sunset, I remove *Avalanche* from my bag and begin to read.

IX

IT'S BEEN FIVE WEEKS SINCE I READ THE BOOK. Maybe more. I'm beginning to lose track of things: time, my dignity, a sense of which way water ought to swirl.

I see Thelma one last time. Out in New Mexico. She surprises me by jumping out from behind a cut-out of a pine tree. Merry Christmas! she cries. She's wearing a Santa Claus bikini and I wonder if maybe it's a dream. She hands me a small gift wrapped in silver paper dotted with pink giraffes. I open it up and find a framed photograph of us sitting on the beach, our backs toward the camera. Between us is a small child, not much more than a baby. All three of us are wearing Santa hats.

Who's that? I ask, pointing at the child. That's our Ollie, she says. You know, from the maybe-times. I kiss her on the forehead. I don't have the heart to tell her the maybe-times will never come.

X

I HAVE A THING TO TELL YOU, the man on the bus whispers in my ear. There are people watching you. You should know about them because we're going to put on a play and the play is about people like me but not like you and you're going to have to leave unless you want to star in the play.

The fields outside lurch past the window and I think to tell the stranger that there aren't fields like this in Philadelphia. I say nothing, but still he nods. That's because you don't remember the city, he says. You have to piece it together from that trip to the museum when you were eight and there was that bomb threat and your father, in his haste to escape great personal harm, pushed you out of the way and down the flight of stairs.

That never happened, I say. That's an exaggeration. Outside, the clouds slip past and I see a billboard of the man with the silver hat eating his Slim Jim, and I think: good for him. Attaboy.

When I turn back to my fellow passenger, he has a bird on his shoulder, a parrot ostentatiously clad in electric green feathers. I'd heard somewhere that animals will speak to you if you listen hard enough. If you ask them with your mind. A friend of mine talked that way with lions once. The things she told me would keep you awake at night. But when I try communicating telepathically with this parrot, he just inches up along the man's shoulder until he's almost next to his ear.

Can't you hear me, Parrot? Can't you? I yell at him with my mind.

He turns and shocks his beady black eyes at me.

Leave me alone! he snaps.

The man holds out his wrist and the bird climbs on top of it and rides it like a little tram over to the left side of the man's body, positioned now to stare out the window at the passing Americana.

I thought you should know, the man says to me, that Aquifer is back with the Tower. The shame was too great, her leaving like that in the middle of the night.

Leaning back in my seat, I feel something sticking out of my pocket and reach back to find the PDX zine. I open it and inside I find a coaster from a bar in Ojai. I gently place it on the floor of the bus, and decide to change my route.

XI

IT'S SUNDAY NIGHT WHEN I MAKE IT BACK to that bar in Ojai. Fauve's sister is there and she's still looking for her. I know from the clock on the wall that no more than a year has gone by, but her eyes look out at me from beneath a face pillaged by time, or maybe by the sun.

You never found her, she says, and then she stubs out into the ashtray what I think must be a cigarette, but when I look closer I see that it's the talon of what must have been a very large bird of prey.

I did, though, I say. I keep finding her. I just can't make her stay.

She shakes her head. Stop fucking around. No more goddamn fucking around. You need to find my sister.

I shrug and light a real cigarette. Do you ever feel like someone is watching us?

I used to, she says, but that stopped when I took up the bottle.

How long ago was that?

She shrugs and stares down at her fingers, clubbed at the end, a sign, I know, of a heart losing its race against time.

I never should have asked you to find anyone. You're ineffectual. A coward.

I found the priest, I protest, though I'm no longer sure if it's true. I'm no longer sure that there ever was a priest. More of a priest-like structure, a faith-losing mirror molecule to my clue-refusing detective, our chiral bodies feral and angling for salvation.

She tries to take a sip of my drink, but I pull it away from her. Why do you need to find your sister so bad anyway?

Blood feud, she says. I need to kill her before she steals my stuff. What stuff? I ask. She shrugs. My purple party dress, she says. And also, you know, my soul. From her pocket she removes a tiny silver bell and gestures toward the corner.

In the corner sits a man with a case of bells. For a moment I think I know him from somewhere else, somewhere significant, and in that memory, he has a bird on his shoulder, but then I remember it was just a cross-town bus in Philadelphia during one of those times when the sky closed over and the city pretended to be New York.

What's this? *Avalanche*? Fauve's sister asks. She's removed the book from my bag and is flipping through it like it might contain secret money.

It's a map to Fauve, I want to say, but instead I say nothing and snatch it back. To distract her, I begin to tell a story about my cat, his fluffy tail, the haruspicy he's fond of practicing with mouse entrails, but all the while I remember a different set of premises—a resisted narrative that someone once tried to tell me. A story about mermaid girls and kitchens.

XII

That one's not yours, says Ermine. I'm sitting across from him in the bar in Ojai. He's sitting beneath a painting of a woman in a dress shaped like an octopus. The inscription reads: *Gone Fishing!*

What's not mine? I ask. The memory?

He shakes his head. The drink.

I look down at a blue drink, a mermaid-shaped toothpick spearing a maraschino cherry.

Ermine opens his palm. You have what I asked for?

I reach in my jacket pocket and with some surprise, produce the bell he once gave me. He opens his case and places it back in the center. I want to take you somewhere, Ermine says, and he closes the case before I can touch any of the bells. I want you to meet someone.

We leave the bar and walk a short distance across the street, through a park with an outdated metal play structure, pock-marked with peeling yellow paint, and up a short incline to a building like a church or a prison, encircled by a low cement wall. We pass through an archway and are met by a tall man with pale eyes like suns sinking into the sea. When I look more closely at his face, I'm almost certain it's the priest, but there's something different about him. And I realize it's just that his face changes each time I read the story.

Go with the chaplain, Ermine says. I'll wait here. I'm about to leave, when he reaches out and grabs my arm. I almost forgot, he says, and then he strikes me, knuckle connecting with zygomatic arch and I feel a crack. That's from Sal Giancana, he says.

I suppose I should have returned the money.

The chaplain is dressed in robes and when he places an arm around my shoulder, I feel unexpectedly calmed. He takes me to an enclosure, the Silver Forest, he calls it. Here the sky is made of silver, he says. You'll see. I thought this place was called Avalanche, I say, and he shakes his head. Some call it Avalanche. Others call it the Silver Forest. It is a place for forgetting so that we might understand.

Outside I see a woman in a plaid shirt with keys strapped to her belt. She's staring at the ground, lost in thought, or looking for something. Her eyes are glazed over, and when I nod to her, she doesn't respond. Is she all right? I ask. She's fine, the chaplain says. Caroline likes to look for hidden structures. She's still seeking the Dutch Alchemist's code, not knowing, of course, that it's already been found.

It has? I ask, not sure what this code is, but knowing it sounds familiar. This, he says, indicating the property, the structure, none of this would exist if we hadn't deciphered the code.
I stare at him a moment. You deciphered it? No, of course not, he laughs. The little projectionaut did. Or he will. He's doing it right now as we speak, which means he's done it before, which means it's already happened, and therefore already been done. So you see, Caroline Mints searches in vain.

Caroline Mints? I think I read a book by her. He fixes his gaze on me. "Art is the shavings seen from above, moving mysteriously on their own." I've heard that before, I say, turning back toward Caroline.

The man takes me by the arm and leads me deeper into the sanctuary. He adjusts his hair, smoothing a lock behind one ear and then he looks deeply into my eyes and begins speaking:

It was without conscience, he says, that I stole down the flight of stairs in the dark last night. Expectant, a strange kind of fury building in my chest, I slid my hand down the smooth grain of the banister and came to stand at the base of the stairs. Work that day had been arduous, though without much feeling of accomplishment. Yesterday Aquifer told me that she was leaving and. although I wanted to find the truth behind her words, when I looked into her eyes, I could see that she too had turned against us. I couldn't fathom why anyone would want to leave the Tower, to leave His grace.

Actions are not something we discuss much here at the Tower. We're focused on intent—on analyzing it, and more than anything else, questioning it—and I often forget that the actions themselves also sometimes have important consequences. But it was an action, and not the intent behind said action, that was of import to Aquifer last night when the swallows had not yet gone to bed. Actions to which she would only peripherally allude that were behind her sudden, and I don't want to say illegal, but certainly un-condoned, departure.

I prayed that He would never know my transgression. It wasn't His wrath I feared. Rather, it was His disapproval. For there was nothing more resilient, more warm and womb-like than the benevolence of His gaze. It is in those moments that one can feel he is truly seen. And when a person is truly seen, that is the only time he can know for certain that he is distinguishable from the great morass that forms around him in the effluvial aether.

Last night in the dark, at the bottom of the steps, the house was quiet. I marched around the corner toward the kitchen with the short measured steps of a child playing at being a soldier, and when I saw that there was a small figure standing there inside that darkness, my heart gave just a little. I should have known it was Aquifer. We'd planned to meet after all, but it's strange the way the size of a person, particularly one with whom you are friendly, but not exactly friends, changes considerably when one meets them unexpectedly in the dark. I would have guessed that she was much taller—maybe five foot seven in boots—but lingering there in the shadows, she was obviously no more than five feet. Her personality, I decided, must be quite a bit taller than she was, her "circumlocational current" flowing out from her at a much faster rate than the rest of us. And it was this thought, this knowledge, that made me realize how deeply saddened I was that she was going, that she felt the need to go.

But this is a thing I've come to understand: lessons, once learned, can be offered up, and in time they can make a space for transcendence. If a person is lucky and if he appeals to a higher power, and if he has a large enough hole in his heart in which to hide the regret he's folded up like an origami crane, things can go on just as they always have even after a violent and unspeakable rupture...Do you understand? he asks.

But she's come back, I assure him. Aquifer's returned. The man with the parrot told me so.

This seems to please him immensely. He slaps me on the back as if to say, why yes, I would like to go fishing with you. Shall we go inside then? he suggests. I want you to meet a woman. A woman of a spring. She wants very much wants to hear about your progress on the case.

In that building like a church or a prison, encircled by that cement wall like a moat, the priest takes me by the hand and leads me under a second archway. We proceed into a candle-lit church that is not a church. Or perhaps it had once been a church and now is something altogether different. Inside the atrium, an unseen chorus wavers and belts. A melody ripe with something like rage.

This is where he came from
This is where he came
When the people all were swept aside
And the animals forgot to exhale
Will it return to the place
That has always forgotten?
Will it return?

Drums swell, occluding the sacred silence I keep between my ears and for that I am thankful. To feel a rage without a knowledge of origin or desire is to question one's legacy and legitimacy all at once.

Inside the apse now, I meet the Woman of the Spring. Holding a lantern, she takes me by the hand and leads me to a low, wooden bench. Her skin is pallid, her features sharp, and her blue eyes look like vessels sunk in a shipwreck graveyard. She tells me to sit down and hands me something cool to drink.

Did you find him? she asks, but I don't know who she means. Guy, she says. You were supposed to find Guy. I look at her and wonder if this is some kind of trick. I don't know how much to give away. I don't understand, I say. Do you work for the Tower? I thought this was...

It doesn't matter what you thought, she says sharply. Did you find Guy?

Sure, I say. Yeah, I found him. And I gave him the photo. She leans in close, and in her eyes I can see galaxies, tombs, crumbling wonders of the sacred multiplicity. And what, my darling, she asks, was the photo of? It was of him, I say as if releasing a great and terrible exhalation from deep inside some yawning chasm.

She exhales as well and nods. Good. Then he's found his way. He's out there now. Out where? I ask, and she raises her arm, bent at the elbow so it projects upward. The mouth of her sleeve falls to the side, exposing her hand, which she moves slowly in tiny circles. Up there, she says. Reaching behind her, she unhooks something, before turning and fastening those eyes on me once again. Are you frightened? she asks as her pendulous garment drops shuddering to the floor. She stands there cloaked now in scales the color of a jaundiced sclera. I look away.

She places a finger to my glabella and I sigh. Unlike my sister, she says, I do not remember my birth, although I have been assured that it was violent and unusual, though not unusually violent. I was rent from my mother's womb only to refuse to breathe, turning petulantly blue in revolt. My father staggered forth and proclaimed me a Sentinel, one brought forth from the void in direct contradiction of nature. Thusly, I was cast out.

If you truly want to find me, she says, you're going to need to go to sleep.

But I don't want to go to sleep. And I don't ever want to find her. Sighing, a whisper of toxic growth about her, she steps back and shakes her head.

I try to stand up, but I feel woozy. I think about Thelma. About that time we drove across the bottom of the country in waves and then zig-zagged along the top in resplendent parallelism. We had a large black dog back then and we nick-named him "For-Keeps" and we rented a boat on a lake with no bottom and inside that boat on top of that lake she sang me a song about a monastic scribe who lived in the forest and the song went like this:

This is what they drank from
This is where they ate
When the people all were swept into the sea
And the animals forgot to exhale
And that great expanse slowly filled with garbage
And with excrement that was almost
forgotten.
Where have you gone?
Why have you forgotten?

I remember then that I'm still renting that house with all the files in it and some version of a woman still sitting on the deck, so I get up and begin to leave, intent on making my way home. I start walking out through the trees that smell like never-ending sadness and like sand and like a place they're not supposed to be. As I walk, I listen to the earth. It is and is not the same earth I left so many years before. Back now in this same strange land, I wander through the woods at night, but find them empty. At the hot springs, the water no longer flows, the animals are silent, and the ground beneath my naked feet moves only in waves. No longer in spirals.

Sometimes we do things like plant trees in a land where they don't belong, thinking they will provide economic relief, but what we don't know is that the trees we thought we were planting were actually their hundred-year-old ancestors, whose wood was hard and sturdy and wise. And what we don't know is that it took a hundred years for them to get that way and this wood of their children is different, immature, soft and brittle, and the spirits inside volatile and non-compliant. And so nothing happens, no money is made, no spirits are sated. And before you know it, you've not just changed the land's general shape and capacity for magic, but now everything smells vaguely of pepper and mint.

I walk up the steps and don't open the door. Instead I go around the side of the house to the front, to that deck with its balcony and its Adirondack chairs and its tulip-dressed stranger. I sit down and lean back, close my eyes, and wait for someone to find me.

fin.

AUTHORS' NOTE

SWERVE was generated with a set of constraints in the spirit of the OULIPO, the Pataphysicians, and others. These constraints included a series of twelve reference texts—from Margaret Cavendish's *The Blazing World* to Lucretius' *De Rerum Natura*. Each of the twelve texts was assigned a geographic location the authors determined relevant to the text. Each text was also assigned a number: 1-12. Then, at the beginning of each chapter, each author would roll a twelve-sided dice to determine which text, and thus which location, their narrative would interplay with for that chapter. Beyond geography, the authors gave themselves maximal flexibility in how the source texts could be roamed—any modality, motif, structure, tone, or element was permissible to engage.

The book was further developed with one other principal narrative adoption—that the attributes of the metaphysical detective novel would give some engine to the framework of the constraints. Thusly, across the distinct sections, characters—and objects—go missing, only to reappear in different guises or varied permutations, while the detective-characters perform something like an indeterminate search across the authors' dice-rolling traversal of shared textual stimuli.

An experiment in reading as much as it is writing, ***SWERVE*** invites the reader to play detective alongside its detectives. We hope you find what we're looking for.

ABOUT THE AUTHORS

Vincent James lives and writes in Colorado. Visit him at FatherFever.com

Rowland Saifi grew up in Brazil, Arkansas, and places in-between before attending Naropa University, the School of the Art Institute of Chicago, and the University of Denver. Other books include *Lit Windows, The Minotaur's Daughter*, and *Karner Blue Estates*. Work has appeared in *Fact-Simile, Newfound Journal, Kneejerk Magazine*, and *The New York Times*. Exhibitions include *Cairo on the Length* a psychogeography of Egypt curated by Amira Hanafi at Spoke Gallery, and *Institutional Garbage*, curated by Caroline Picard and Lara Schoorl at Hyde Park Arts Center.

McCormick Templeman is the author of *The Little Woods* (Random House) and *The Glass Casket* (Penguin Random House). A graduate of Reed college, she holds a PhD from the University of Denver. She lives in the Pacific Northwest where she is currently lurching about in search of Bigfoot. (Photo credit: Phoebe Camp)

ACKNOWLEDGEMENTS

Vincent James

Vincent James wishes to thank Z, his children, his family, his inlaws, out-laws, teachers, saints, and ne'er do wells for carrying his torch when it reached the embers.

Rowland Saifi

Thank you: duncan b. barlow, Ed Bowes, Kelli Connell, Tristan Duke, Álvaro Enrigue, Jon Fullmer, Stew Glosup, Jaime Groetsema, Hal Hlavinka, Joanna Howard, Scott Howard, Laird Hunt, Vincent James, Kevin Kilroy, Brian Kiteley, Alicia Mountain, Josh Munson, Thirii Myint, Beth Nugent, Pamela Odeh, Emily Pettit, David Ray, Patty Reid, Natalie Rogers, Alana Romund, Seth Rowland, Joanna Ruocco, Adam Smith, Dennis Sweeney, McCormick Templeman, Khadijah Queen, and Anne Waldman.

McCormick Templeman

Thanks to Mona Awad, duncan b. barlow, James Camp, Jocelyn Camp, Phoebe Camp, Quill Camp, Julie Caplan, Camille DeAngelis, Jaime Groetsema, Rachel Feder, Leslie Good, Patricia Hernandez, Joanna Howard, Scott Howard, Laird Hunt, Vincent James, Amy Keys, Brian Kiteley, Kristen Kittscher, Brian Laidlaw, Larry Lillvik, Mark Mayer, Suzanne Motley, Alicia Mountain, Thirii Myint, Emily Pettit, Khadijah Queen, Brooke Rogers, Natalie Rogers, Rowland Saifi, Selah Saterstrom, Dennis J. Sweeney, Kathi Templeman, Ted Templeman, Alison Turner, Andrew Wille, and the late Keith Abbott, who taught me pretty much everything I know.